The Woodcarver's Hand

by Amber Taylor-Pengov

Outskirts Press, Inc.
Denver, Colorado

This is a work of fiction. The events and characters described here are imaginary and are not intended to refer to specific places or living persons. The opinions expressed in this manuscript are solely the opinions of the author and do not represent the opinions or thoughts of the publisher. The author represents and warrants that s/he either owns or has the legal right to publish all material in this book. If you believe this to be incorrect, contact the publisher through its website at www.outskirtspress.com.

The Woodcarver's Hand
All Rights Reserved
Copyright © 2005 Amber Taylor-Pengov

This book may not be reproduced, transmitted, or stored in whole or in part by any means, including graphic, electronic, or mechanical without the express written consent of the publisher except in the case of brief quotations embodied in critical articles and reviews.

Outskirts Press
http://www.outskirtspress.com

ISBN: 1-59800-014-4

Library of Congress Catalog Number: 2005926222

Outskirts Press and the "OP" logo are trademarks belonging to
Outskirts Press, Inc.

Printed in the United States of America

*For my father,
a man who is fighting his own battle every day.*

Prologue

Twenty-one years after experiencing the death of her parents, Gail sits in her office, reflecting upon the series of events that led her to the life she now leads. Within her hands, she holds a small black diary containing her life's most treasured moments. Gail knows that each sacred memory is worth sharing in order to spare another soul.

In her heart, she believes every soul has a story to be told. If each man listens carefully enough, he can hear the creator telling the tale of his character's journey to self-discovery. Without the creator's hand, a character's soul can never exist.

2004 Diary: twenty-one years after death

With each man's first breath of life comes a new story to be told over time. As infants, every new curiosity steals the innocence from within our soul. As the world undergoes constant development around us, we as individuals grow and learn to walk forward through time as well. As a result of our travels, adventurous tales of epic triumphs and disastrous stories of misfortunes begin to unfold, while following us throughout the length of our life's journey. With each turn of our stories' pages, our minds become engrossed by the breathtaking events that spin and spiral about us; consequently, our eyes continuously learn to unravel the clues to our distant future.

Each step taken further into our future adds a new line to every paragraph of our lives. As the plot unfolds, we encounter many obstacles. With every battle won or lost, a scar is received. Whether the scar remains physically visible or hidden as an emotional wound, it builds our character into the defined individual we are destined to become.

Nobody knows how many steps it will take to complete a chapter in our character's life or how many obstacles we will overcome along our journey. All I know is that I have learned that this life is only the beginning. After we leave this world, there is an eternity waiting beyond our realm of imagination. And with every waking day, we have traveled a little closer to our heaven.

The only question worth asking ourselves every morning is whether or not we can accept the hand that turns the pages of our life. Do you as an individual believe in the hand of your creator?

Once I was a loner in the shadows of forgotten days and nights, haunted by the ghosts of time that once plagued my life. Now I share my tale of triumphs for the future of tomorrow's souls.

Chapter One

"'Open your eyes and free your mind from its darkened depths of your prison. Once your mind has been freed from the dark, the light to your heart will soon chase the shadows away. As the sun showers warmth upon man, this new light will wrap its arms around your heart and open doors to new possibilities. These new possibilities will present ideas that will allow you to question your purpose. The answers to these questions will be revealed once you understand the truth behind your life...the truth that lies in the woodcarver's hand.'"

A hint of a smile crept across my quivering lips as I read aloud the words printed upon the paper before my eyes. With each word recollected in thought, reflected memories were summoned into my wandering mind:

She could vividly hear her grandfather's words rattling within her mind as she watched him carve in admiration. Her eyes brilliantly glowed in the light of the embers, while she watched him grip the carving wood tightly within his left hand. Her body could still feel the warmth emitted by the roaring fire. Its flames, flickering within the heat, seemed to dance with each piece of whittled wood that fell upon them by her grandfather's precious hands.

No matter how hard Gail tried not to stare, she could not help but gaze into his crystal blue eyes. All it took was one glance, and she became captivated by their radiant appearance. For his sapphire eyes never moved from his creation, not even when he spoke. And she never once saw his hand rest from motion until his creation was complete and perfect through his own vision.

"It can never be perfect, Grandpa," she told him.

"No, probably not to you. Yet, to the maker, every detail was completely planned out and carved with thought; therefore, there can never be any imperfection," he replied, as he held his creation up to light with a brilliant smile hidden beneath the gray scruff upon his old chin.

"But if that is a rendition of me, it will never be perfect," she commented, and robbed him of his glorious moment.

"Gail, of all your faults, I have never found any that would make me love you any less, so this carving of you could never be less than perfect," he returned, with a single tear upon his cheek, and still his eyes never strayed from his carved creation.

"Grandpa..." she uttered in tears, and wrapped her arms tightly around him. She understood the grievance he possessed within his heart, but before that moment, he had never revealed the bottled emotion as she had many times before.

"You remind me so much of him," Noah whispered within her ear. "I wish we could have continued our lives together,

all of us. Sometimes I just don't understand why there couldn't have been another way."

"I will never leave you," she cried in the hope that he would never leave me either, but she knew it wasn't possible to live forever, especially not with the disease her grandfather had already been coping with for years.

"Do not make promises that you cannot keep, child," he remarked, as he pulled her body away from his chest in order to see her face. "You never know where your journey will take you or when it will end."

"But Grandpa..."

"Shh! Just promise me that no matter where you go, you will always understand who you are and where you are going in life. Then, discover the reason why things have to be the way they are. Do it for me," he urged, as the tears stopped flowing from his eyes, and the fire's light began to fade. Gail just sat and watched. She watched his face in silence until it was completely dimmed by the disappearing life within the fire's dying glow.

Finally, when the light had completely vanished from view, I found myself standing alone before our family and friends. My eye's desperately fought to maintain control as I focused my attention back on the crowd before me. I quickly followed my grandfather's words back to the beginning, but my grieving soul took precedence over my wishes. With a deep breath, my lungs forced my lips to release the dreaded cry from its captive cell. My shaking hand released the iron-tight grip it had applied to my grandfather's note and inconspicuously wiped the tears escaping from my swollen brown eyes. In one quick motion, I closed my eyes tightly until the pain subduing my body was slowly breathed away.

Reluctantly reopening them, I found myself staring profoundly into the expressions that were cast by my family and friends. Their comforting sighs and consenting sobs provided the confidence I sought in order to continue my speech, but I could no longer let them see me cry or sob in painful emotion. Inside my heart, I believed I was stronger than they were. I could handle anything that crossed my path. I did not want their pity or their comfort. It was they who needed consolation from me. After all, I had plenty of practice in pretending not to be pained by the death of a loved one.

"I'm not exactly sure what my grandfather meant by his words," I finally revealed, "but I do know that he left them behind for us to learn from their meaning. My grandfather was an explorer and traveler for truth, knowledge, and understanding. What he learned, he taught to others who crossed his path. Except, Noah never left you with a moral to his lessons. Instead, he expected you to discover the truth on your own.

"I believe that my grandfather is challenging us to discover who we really are and daring us to embrace ourselves from within. He knew in his heart that each of us is carved out by another being..."

I paused for a brief moment and reflected upon the words entrapped in my heart. I smiled at my thoughts and added, "Noah used to say, 'Within a lifetime, God presents man with many different paths. The path man desires may not be the one that God has chosen for him, but until he locates his chosen path, he'll never become who he is meant to be in life. He'll never understand why the path he is on keeps spinning in circles and why the story is always ending in the same manner.'

"He also used to say, 'Man should always learn to take less; that way he can be sure to gain more in the end.' I'm not real clear on what Noah meant by those words, but I do know that before his death, he told me that he had gained more in his lifetime than he ever expected, and he had taken nothing from those who were not willing to give it to him freely.

"When he spoke these words to me, I had never been more proud of him before that very moment. For him to accept the man he had become is a difficult task alone. Yet, not only did he have faith in himself, he believed in what he had accomplished within his lifetime. To believe in yourself and in your dreams is a demanding path for any human to follow, and he managed to do both. So with that in mind, I know that even within his death, his journey will continue forward," I concluded, with confidence in my voice but deceit in mind.

I lied.

Standing before my family and friends, during my own grandfather's funeral—the funeral of the very man who raised me—I flat-out lied. I didn't believe he continued on. I definitely didn't understand why he was taken from me when I had never taken anything from anyone. I had not gained anything. I only discovered how it felt to be robbed of everything I had ever loved.

"Why shouldn't I be angry?" she thought to herself the day of the funeral. Yet, she could not accept the guilt and shame of the lie she told her family. It seemed to be eating her alive.

So, like a child, I sat and pouted in the distance. I watched as everyone said their final good-byes and comforted each other in their time of hurt and suffering. I could not find any pity for them. Even as they gathered in groups to pray and console each other, I could not find an ounce of sympathy stored in my heart. Though they had known him their entire lives, they were not the ones who lost a piece of everything they had ever known.

He was the only father she could recollect.

Eventually, the crowd before me slowly faded into the oncoming dusk. It seemed like only moments before the sun filtered over my eyes and the grief-stricken faces of each of the parting mourners. Its peaceful warmth enchanted my soul and filtered through my judgmental eyes.

Solemnly, my gaze turned back toward my grandfather's limp body, which lay helplessly in the cold, metal casket. His gray hair flapped in the strawberry breeze that flowed through from the nearby field. The sweet smell, accompanied by the warmth of the setting sun, helped me realize how grateful I was to be alive and free.

As the last griever departed, I was left hovering alone over my grandfather's body. I clenched my jaw until the unbearable pain broke the seal and allowed a faint sob to protrude past my lips. My blood jabbed at my weeping heart, causing it to throb in agony. I could feel the salt stains building on the edge of my tearing eyes. With a bursting bawl of emotions, I flooded the casket with every ounce of agony I contained.

The last memory she had of her grandfather was of him floating away in the tears she shed. Yet, it comforted her to know that a part of her would always remain with him.

"Hey, are you okay?" came a voice from behind my back, as a hand was placed peacefully upon my stiffened shoulders. As my muscles cringed with a startle, my body awoke to the reality surrounding me. I quickly remembered who possessed the friendly hand.

"Have you ever lied to anyone you loved, Damien?" I asked, without expecting an answer to an obvious question, but still he thought my question over with careful consideration. He didn't seem to want to say anything wrong.

"Are you talking about your eulogy?" he finally asked, in response to my question. He had always felt the way I did about life after death; perhaps he doubted even more so.

"I know that it is wrong to lie. But how can words be a lie if they are not meant to hurt anyone but only comfort another individual's grieving soul?" I asked, as I tried to persuade myself into believing what I had said during my grandfather's funeral was a lie with good intentions.

"It was a white lie," Damien comforted, as we watched the groundskeepers shovel the earth back into its rightful place.

"It is strange how when we die, we are lowered back into where it was that we came from," I said aloud.

"C'mon, Gail, it is time for us to go home," Damien said, as he tried to ignore my comment. "Anneal is waiting for us in the car."

"Well, why didn't they come, Damien? They could have at least come to his funeral," I mentioned, in response to my brother's suggestion of saying our final good-byes to our grandfather. By the look planted upon his face, I could tell that he had expected my comment.

"I know that, but they didn't. Just get over it," he replied, with a distasteful tone in his harshening voice.

"Even in death they could not accept his decision. It isn't right."

"No, it isn't! But I cannot do anything to change that, and neither can you!" he declared.

"We have nobody left, Damien. What is the matter with this family?" I bellowed out in anger, as the fear in my rage could no longer be caged. "What are we going to do?"

"I do not know," he answered calmly. "It just seems that they wanted us dead instead of them."

The tears began to roll from my eyes and down my flesh.

They streamed from the bottom of my lip and dripped upon the grassy soil lying beneath my feet. In only a few precious seconds, the tears were gone. They had been swallowed by the ground's thirst.

I slowly looked up from the ground and away from the gravesite. In the distance, my eyes caught a glimpse of movement. I blinked rapidly, desperately trying to wash away my blurred vision. Before my eyes could focus on the mysterious figure in the shade of the shadow's setting sun, it was gone. It had disappeared into the woodland area surrounding the graveyard.

"What is it, Gail?" Damien asked, as he followed my gaze with his eyes.

"I don't know. I thought that I saw someone over there."

"I don't see anything important. All that I see is a deer over there."

"What deer?" I asked, searching the tree line.

"Right there. Do you see him? It looks like a fawn," he concluded. "It must be a good sign about our grandfather. The deer was always one of his favorite animals."

"Probably," I agreed with doubt. "Let's go home now."

Gail will never be able to forget any of the experiences of that day. And she won't understand how much the event affected her until later within her life.

She will always be able to taste the sweetness of spring upon her tongue as it mixes with the bitterness of death. She will never be able to forget the feel of love stirring within her soul each time the warmth of the sun dances upon the cold chill of her skin. And till the end of her days, she will remember the lovely scent of daisies swaying in the wind as the smell of decay is pushed beneath the hollow ground. And her mind will never be able to forget the sound of the birds chirping a joyous melody in a time of sorrow. She always will remember how the birds sang with delight as if they were oblivious to death. All of these conditions will eventually help her to remember how life always goes on with or without her. But for now, until a better opportunity arises, she will question life and the truth behind death.

Diary: The passing

30 May, 03

Jeremiah 29:11 "For I know the plans I have for you," declares the Lord, "plans to prosper you and not to harm you, plans to give you hope and the future."

As I walk through this life, I find myself wondering about our purpose. Why should man's existence continue to prosper through time? Have we fulfilled our expectations and done all that could be hoped for? If so, why should we have to die to live? And why must some suffer in the end?

Though my grandfather died a death that destroyed him from the inside, he never doubted his faith. He never lost his faith in the Lord the creator. How could a dying man believe in something so strongly? Was it fear, or was it that he understood more than the rest of the dying souls in this world can comprehend?

Chapter Two

The morning sun stretched out its arms to pull back the curtain on my bedroom window. It slowly peeked through the curtain and crept inside the bedroom. Settling down next to me, it crawled beneath the covers and wrapped its welcoming arms around my body. Bashfully, the sun blushed with embarrassment and quickly withdrew its rays from my rousing body. Instead, it showered its comfortable, cozy feeling about the room and raced back to my nose in order to tickle me awake.

Grumpily, with a fuss and a scratch of my nose, I turned upon my side to sleep off the day. Yet out of nowhere, a smile suddenly spread across my tired face as if the sun had chased away every thought that had entered my mind. I felt fresh and free. My body seemed to come alive with the touch of the sun.

For that one cherished moment, I felt as young and free as

a child again. Everything in my life seemed to be released from my imprisoned heart. Yet, as the sun faded and hid behind the approaching clouds to play peek-a-boo with the day, I heard the present reality snicker its way back from beyond. A sharp pain at the base of my jaw jabbed at my thoughts, causing me to wince as it raced throughout my body like the disappearance of a thousand years fading into history without a story to tell.

She closed her eyes, wishing and longing to feel that childhood wholeness again, but nothing came back to her heart. The desire to become whole again plagued at her soul until it echoed throughout her body. The sound of the echo cursed her mind without any fear.

Slowly rising to my feet with another grunt and a groan, I breathed away the agonizing pain in my life. The thoughts of yesterday's funeral began to brutally attack my mind with visions of death. I could not escape them. Each horrific thought continued to vividly float throughout the room, lunging at me with every step that I took forward. My mind could not fathom the possible meaning of such dreadful thoughts. Within moments, the thoughts of yesterday transpired into fears of the attacking future.

Knock! Knock! came a bang from the other side of the door. Fearing it was death knocking at my door, I lunged back into bed in order to pretend that I was still resting peacefully. Just before throwing myself into a panic attack, my mind was put to rest by the sound of a familiar friend's voice. "I was just wondering what you wanted for breakfast this morning? I don't mind fixing something."

It was Anneal. She had been my best friend since I was five. I can hardly remember a day without her. If there was something I needed, she was always more than willing to help, especially during times of remorse. Though she meant well, there were some instances when I found her to be overbearing.

When she asked me about breakfast that morning, I didn't really care much for eating. The thought of food repulsed me. How could I go on living life after the death of a man that I felt living without would completely destroy me? I couldn't function without him. In a way, I wished it had been death instead of Anneal. I was quite certain that I would have let it take me away without much of a fight.

"Well," she replied, when I didn't offer an answer, "just get yourself cleaned up, and I will have something waiting for you."

Did she mean shower? Gail asked herself. Showering meant that she would be washing away the events of yesterday, which in return meant that she would be washing away her grandfather. She wasn't completely ready to wash him from her life, but she also knew wasting away to nothing would not heal her pain. She knew it was best for her to continue caring for the things she had left in her life. She felt that she had learned that much from her grandfather before he passed away and left her alone.

"Hey, good morning," Anneal said, when I finally decided to join her for breakfast. "How are you feeling?"

"How do you think I feel?" I rudely snapped, and slumped onto the kitchen chair placed at the table. My eyes kept wandering from the stove to the hallway before the living room. Someone was missing. I knew they would never step through that doorway again, but at the same time, I kept hoping to be proved wrong. All I wanted was to see my grandpa's smiling face cooking me breakfast one last time. He was such a wonderful cook.

"Well, you smell clean, and your clothes match. I think that is a pretty good start," she answered.

Disgusted with her lighthearted and carefree attitude, I contentiously asked, "What did you make me for breakfast?"

"Aren't we a bit grouchy?" she snapped back, with a roll and flicker of her eyes. "Anyway, I made something that would fill up everyone's hungry tummies. I made..."

"I'm not a kid, Anneal," I reminded her. "Just tell me what you made, and quit asking how I feel. I just lost the only family I had left. It is a stupid question to ask someone after a funeral."

Sighing, she briskly walked to the refrigerator in stride and pulled out a plate of blueberry waffles, which were smothered in raspberry syrup and topped off with whipped cream and a cherry.

"Enjoy!" she remarked, as she plopped the plate upon the table. "You are not the only one who is hurting," she scolded.

"Hey," Damien called, as he walked into the room, "take it easy, babe."

"Tell that to your ungrateful sister," she rebuked, and stormed out of the room.

"What is her problem?" he asked me, while dipping his finger into my whipped cream.

"She thinks she has a right to be more upset than I do, and I won't acknowledge her prissy little attitude," I answered obstinately.

"This is really good," he replied, referring to the waffles. "I hope she made some for me, too."

Turned off by Damien's reaction to the entire situation, I decided to leave the table. In a childish manner, I brushed past his shoulder and stomped into the living room.

"Where are you going?" he called to my back.

"You're an idiot!" I shouted over my shoulder.

"So are you going to eat this?" he shouted to me, while I raced about the living room in order to find and collect the belongings I needed for the workday.

Throwing on my jacket, I stuck my head through the doorway of the kitchen and said, "I am going to work. Are you coming?"

"I'll be there. What car are you taking?"

"Mine," I unpleasantly answered, knowing exactly what his question was leading toward.

"I was just thinking that you could take Grandpa's truck today, and I could take your jeep."

"No! I'm not driving Grandpa's car. Give the guy a chance to be dead!" I shouted at him. "And if you had fixed the stupid brakes in your car from the beginning, you would have your own car to drive!"

"Gail, I didn't mean anything by asking you to drive it today! If you are leaving without me, I still need a car to drive," he explained.

"I'm going to work," I bluntly informed him.

"So what did we decide here?" he naively asked.

Pretending not to hear him, I walked through the living room to the front door and let it slam behind my back. Just outside the door, I was stopped by Anneal, who was rocking steadily upon the porch swing.

Shocked, she asked, "You are going to work?"

"I'm going to work," I said, and stepped down the top stair leading away from our home.

"You can't go to work," she insisted, and let her stomping foot clamor against the hollow porch.

"Anneal, it is the only place that I feel I can be right now without being reminded of him."

"I was just thinking that it would be a good idea for all of us to take some time off right now. Maybe we could just get away for a bit."

Feeling bad about my approach toward her earlier, I

stepped back upon the porch and gingerly sat down next to her on the swing. The hurt in her eyes could clearly be seen.

"Anneal, I'm sorry I was so rude to you. It was really nice of you to make breakfast. I just feel that nobody cares about him being gone. Everybody wants to go on as if nothing ever happened. You can't do that. You can't bottle everything up inside."

"Of course we care. We are just trying not to think about how much it hurts."

"But we can't pretend it didn't happen."

"We aren't pretending. I think Damien and I just grieved a long time ago. We knew it was going to happen eventually."

"It just seemed as though he would live forever, you know? I mean, I knew he would die eventually, but I didn't think he would go the way he did. He seemed so strong, almost like an immortal."

"He is immortal now. I am sure of it," she stated.

Gail didn't believe it, though. In her mind, she kept arguing with herself. She didn't want to say it out loud. She knew how strongly Anneal felt about the afterlife.

"I'm not sure I believe that," I finally admitted.

"What?" squealed Anneal. "Yesterday, at the funeral, you said that you were sure that he lived on."

"I know what I said, but I didn't really believe it. I just said it because everybody wanted me to say it."

"Oh, Gail. Why didn't you say something? Maybe we should talk about this?"

"Uh, not now!" I sharply replied, with a shrug of my shoulders. "I'm going to be late as it is."

"This is just not something you can walk away from. You are going to have to face reality some day."

"It is your reality. Not mine," I argued. "Anyway, I need

to go. The kids need me right now. I'm sure they are upset about Noah's death, too. They may not want to continue with the summer kick-off, and I think that it would be better if we did. It will ease everyone's emotions, and I think Noah would want it that way."

"And what are you going to tell them when they ask if Noah is with God? It is a Christian-based camp, Gail."

"I don't know. I will think of something. I always do."

"Gail, you should really stay home," she argued.

"Or not," I said, and began to walk off the porch once again, but I didn't want to leave with Anneal thinking I had forgotten about her needs and feelings. I did understand that she was experiencing the loss as well, but it just didn't seem to be to the same degree of magnitude as my pain. "Oh, I almost forgot to ask. How is 'Noah's Ark' going?"

"I think the animals know that he is gone," she sighed, but she seemed relieved that I had asked her about the situation. "They really miss him. They keep looking at the doorway as if he is going to walk in any second. I think they feel like he has forgotten them."

"I know how they feel," I stated clearly. Eventually, after I was positive the meaning of my statement had thoroughly sunk in to Anneal, I asked, "What about a new head veterinarian? Dr. Temper is going to be leaving soon."

"Still looking," she answered, with a slight shrug of her shoulders. "I honestly don't know if we will find anyone in time."

Chapter Three

"**I** don't think I can do this," said the young boy dangling from the blue bungee cord with his body tightly coiled. His oversized maroon helmet barely left room for his tiny eyes to peek through. Bobbing up and down, he looked like an out-of-sync yo-yo.

"Yes, you can do this," I tried to persuade. "Just keep kicking your legs until you can swing over and reach the log."

"I can't. It is too far! I am going to fall!" he cried, while kicking his feet about as if he were in a fit of rage.

"C'mon, you are making us lose!" shouted another child behind my back.

"I told you that we should not have put him up there. The kid is a chicken sh..."

"Hey!" I shouted, cutting Peter off. "The reason I put him up there is because he is the smallest, not because he is the bravest or the strongest. He will have an easier time climbing through the ropes, and he'll have much better balance than anyone else because of his size. Now give him a chance," I pleaded with the other children. After explaining my reasoning to the rest of the group, I turned my attention back to the frightened boy suspended above us. "Davy, you need to pump your legs like you are on a swing."

"Okay, I am trying!" he whined, whipping his legs back and forth.

He wasn't trying very hard. Gail knew he could do much better. She was beginning to grow very frustrated with him, and the rest of the children in her group were vividly reading her emotions.

"Davy, try harder!" I shouted at him. I began to realize that Anneal might have been right about staying home. I really didn't have much patience for the children that day. I was even more upset with the fact that most of them didn't even care about Noah's death. They never even questioned me about him.

"This is absolutely ridiculous!" Peter whined. "Even you feel that this is hopeless."

"Peter!" I shouted, and threw him a glance of warning.

"Just shut up! Just shut up! Everyone just needs to shut up!" Gail screamed from inside of her mind.

"Hey! The players on the other teams fell, too. I think they are too big for this part of the relay!" Samantha informed the team.

"Oh, really. I think I told you guys that from the beginning!" she pointed out to herself.

"Come on! Davy, now is your chance!" the team cried with hope.

"Argh," he groaned, as he swung his legs back and forth. He rocked and pumped harder than I had ever seen him try before. In seconds, he was swinging gracefully in the air!

The Woodcarver's Hand

His tiny hand caught the rope attached to the log as the other children coaxed him forward. They cheered gleefully as his feet swooped upon the log beneath the rope his fingers clutched. Hand over hand, foot over foot, and rope over rope, Davy made his way through his part of the course. His wide smile grinned happily at us.

The group tournaments were held once a year, every year. It always fell toward the end of spring. It was a tribute to the approaching summer fun that always occurred at the recreation camp.

The camp was created by my grandfather and his son, my father. They called it "The Lantern." Noah eventually passed the camp onto Damien and me at the ages of 21 and 18. Of course, we accepted and left him to run "Noah's Ark," his heart's true passion.

From the time we inherited the camp, Damien and I had not changed one rule about the tournament. The object of the relay was obvious—to win. The idea was to be the lead cabin for the approaching summer. There were four cabins total. Each cabin held 20 children with two counselors, one male and one female.

The course was basically the same each year but set up backwards, with beginning and end in different locations. Each child was selected to complete an area of the course. Once his hands and feet crossed the red-marked lines in his section, the next teammate could begin his part.

We'd already scaled the rock wall, jumped through the tires, crawled through the tunnels, and captured one of our team's yellow flags when Davy's turn had arrived.

After Davy had completed his section, it was Betty's turn to climb up the cargo net, cross the balance beam, and glide down the trapeze in order to plunge into the pond beneath her. After that, she had to pass the one yellow flag onto Diane, who was waiting patiently to swim out and grab the second yellow flag. Then, Diane had to swim over to Toby, Keith, and Melissa, who were waiting patiently in a canoe. Once they received both flags, the three of them paddled across the lake and around the buoys. Once they reached the other side of the lake, they grabbed the third and final flag and raced to where Damien was waiting by the archery area. He assisted them in attaching each flag onto one arrow apiece. First Toby shot, then Melissa, and finally Keith took his turn. Keith was the only one to hit the bull's-eye. In fact, he was the only one out of the whole camp.

As a result, even though our team finished the relay in third place, they still won. By pinning the flag to a bull's-eye, our team was allowed to collect enough points to squeak past the first-place cabin.

Ecstatic, the children cried, "Yeah, we did it! We won! We won!"

Their gloating made Gail's stomach turn sour. She was shocked by their joy of winning. It was difficult for her to find happiness in winning by default. More important, she was saddened by the fact that this would be the first year her grandfather would not be around to present the winner with the golden trophy. Not one child seemed to care that he was not around anymore.

For moments on end, she stood in agitated silence. Her world seemed to be spinning out of control, and she had not prepared her body for the chaotic ride. At any moment, she felt as if the life she knew would be torn from her body, and she would be left spinning alone for an eternity of Hell.

"Hey, guys, calm down!" I ordered and reminded them, "Everyone in the camp will still get the pizza and ice cream, so you don't have to be that excited."

"We know about the food," Peter remarked, "but we are

the youngest group here, and we get to boss everyone around this summer!"

"Yeah, we get to tell them what they have to do this year," Betty added.

"No, no," I commented, "you get to choose the order in which they participate in the events. The counselors will decide on what events take place."

"Whatever! Same difference!" they said together.

"What does that mean?" I asked. "One win and you think you are on top of the world."

"Aren't you excited that we won?" questioned a voice from behind us.

It was Damien. Like the children, he was overjoyed by the fact that our cabin had won. He kept jumping up and down, while rubbing his greedy hands together. His behavior kept riling the group's egos even more.

"We won by a technicality," I remarked.

"Yeah, but you did a good job getting Davy to finish his part. I could hear you all the way across the lake," he added.

Still bothered by the win and their resulting behavior, just for spite, I said, "We should change that rule. Dad and Noah are the ones who made it up anyway. Neither of them is even here anymore. So what difference would it make?"

"What?" Damien asked in an irritated manner. "You can't change the rules after the fact, Gail. Besides, just because they are dead, it doesn't mean that we should change everything they worked hard to gain. Plus, it is a good rule."

"I just think that we should add a little variety to the course so that we could spice it up a little, ya know? You shouldn't have to lose if you finished the race first."

"It gives everyone a chance to win. The older guys would wipe the floor with these little guys."

"So what? That is life. They will learn that, eventually.

Someday when they are the big kids, they will do the same thing to the new little guys.

"We were given this camp to run, and there should be some changes made. We should have done it before. I just thought it would hurt Grandpa's feelings. Now that he is gone, we can do what we want," I decided, but I really didn't want to change anything. I liked the way the camp was run. I just kept thinking that it wouldn't hurt so much if we changed everything that reminded me of my grandfather.

"Excuse me?" Damien sounded.

"What if he comes back?" Diane asked.

"He isn't coming back, sweetie," Damien stated.

"Why?"

"Because he is dead," I commented without remorse. "At least I can acknowledge his death. Everyone else pretends it never happened."

"Gail!" Damien screamed.

"What?" I ignorantly asked, while looking around at the faces of the children and said, "It is true. He does the same thing with our parents. He completely ignores the fact that we have family in another part of this state, too."

"Gail!" Damien shouted at me, as he raced toward me in fury. "Just shut your mouth! Just shut up!"

Suddenly, Gail realized that no one was excited about the pizza and ice cream anymore. Some of the other counselors were trying to calm down the sobbing children. Other children were being removed from the area by the rest of the staff.

"Oh, no! What have we done?" I asked Damien

"Gail? Damien?" the camp counselor, Susan, from the teenager's cabin called aloud to us. "Maybe the two of you should take some time off. We can handle things for a bit. I just don't think you are ready to be here."

"No," I remarked, "Damien is handling everything just fine by pretending Noah never existed. He just doesn't like how it sounds coming from me, so I think I should be the one to go. I can't be here right now with all this pretending nothing happened stuff!"

Chapter Four

*H*ome was 40 miles from the "The Lantern." All Gail had to do was pass through the city and drive west for about another 20 miles. With each passing mile, her heart sank deeper into the pit of her stomach. All the commotion within the city's wall had only heightened her raging anger. Its polluted air had traveled through the blood in her veins like the poison of an addicting drug. The frustration felt by each passerby on the street only pumped the drug further into the blood of her heart.

"God, you idiot!" Gail shouted in rage, as she pressed her hand firmly on the blaring horn of the jeep. "Watch where you are going!" she said angrily, directing her words to the young, slick man in his convertible as he flew past her with his music trailing behind him.

Gail was unable to control her rage and unwilling to swallow her pride. Everyone around her was being *completely insensitive to what she had just been through. She couldn't wait to arrive on the other side of the city, but once the time came, she lost any relief that had stemmed from the root of her burning rage. A shadow of doubt filtered over her hope, causing it to wither and die. She knew what lay on the opposite side of the city, and she wasn't sure she could travel past it alone.*

After the rage brewing inside had been subdued by fear, Gail quickly rethought her position and decided that it might have been better to remain behind the protection of the city's walls.

Chapter Five

The air in the cemetery was staler than it had appeared the day of the funeral. There weren't any strawberry breezes in the nearby field. Only the smell of decay lingered from the rotten corpses lying beneath my feet.

Not a word was spoken, nor a noise heard. She began to think that it was quiet enough for the dead to hear her footsteps approaching. She wondered if they knew she was coming. She was certain that after awhile they could recognize the different sounds that a person made when they walked. What else did the dead have to do? All they could do was lie alone for an eternity, perhaps completely alone if they never had any visitors.

"Hey, Grandpa. How is it going..."

"How is it going? You don't ask a dead person that. How do you think it is going?" she argued with herself.

"Today has been kind of awful..."

"Like his day has been so much better than yours, idiot!"
She was beginning to think that talking to the dead was going to be more difficult than she first imagined.

"Look, I'm not really good at this. I feel kind of strange doing this in the first place, so I'm just going to fill you in on what happened today.

"First, I completely came down hard on Anneal. She was just trying to help everyone out. She wasn't trying to hurt anyone. I just felt like she didn't care that you were gone. She just kept going about her same old routine. Then, Damien and I got into this huge argument about how to run the camp. It wouldn't have been so bad if we hadn't fought in front of the children. By the time we were through, we had most of them in tears. It was supposed to be a happy day for them, but I ruined it because I can't handle the fact that you are gone. So, I left the camp and came here to see you...talk to you. Oh, on the way over here, some young punk cut me off and didn't even acknowledge what he had done!

"I guess what I am trying to say is that everything is a mess without you. I just don't know how to handle anything without you. I feel like I am a child all over again and learning about life for the first time. I need some help. You always have the best advice. So if there is anything you can do to help me, I would really appreciate it."

Crack! Snap!

A large crackling noise sounded from the nearby wooded area surrounding me, but as I glanced about the cemetery, there wasn't a single object, other than brumous clouds of gray overcasting graves of dismay, in sight for my eyes to visualize.

She quickly began to imagine the dead coming back to life. She figured that she must have disturbed their eternal sleep, and now they were coming to silence her! Soon, they would be climbing out of their graves in order to pull her beneath the soil, so that her flesh could rot with them! What was she going to do? There was nobody around to save her!

Pop! Snap! Crack!

"Oh, God!" I shouted and jumped to my feet. "Hello? Is somebody there?"

Rustle, rustle, slur, slur!

Came the noises again as she whirled back around and dashed behind her grandfather's towering tombstone in order to seek shelter, but just as she was about to hide, she was stopped by the creature sneaking up behind her back!

"Phew!" I sighed. I realized that it was only a young deer, the same young deer that Damien and I had encountered the day of the funeral. She was very young and beautiful. Her entire body was covered in a smooth, sleek coat of brown and white. She was probably the only thing radiating with pure white light throughout the cemetery.

Boldly, I stepped closer to the young fawn, but she was gone by the time I had completed my first step closer to her. She raced with the speed of nature. She knew she was too quick for me to keep up, so she ran and ran until she saw her mother in the distance. With one quick agile bound into the air, she turned and raced toward her mother with wild spirit. Her mother just watched her gallop with pride, and in an instant, she turned for her daughter to follow her into the wild.

Suddenly, I noticed that she had changed her direction and was headed directly toward the main road. I knew she was not going to make it. There was a large white semi-truck rapidly approaching. I knew I could not catch up to them, but I wanted to help.

How could she warn them? It was impossible, so she just closed her eyes and gritted her teeth until the squealing brakes could not be heard in the distance.

"No!" I screamed in horror, when I saw the body of the helpless doe lying in the middle of the road. I kept searching the tree line, but the young fawn was nowhere to be seen. The poor thing had to watch as her mother was nearly killed by a truck driver who never even stopped to help.

"Somebody help!" I called, as I rushed to the doe's aid. She was lying helpless along the berm. I never thought that anyone could hear me or would bother to help.

But she was wrong. Somebody had been watching her.

"Let me help you!" a strange man urged, as he raced out of the woods.

His dark eyes pierced mine as I examined his dirt-washed face. The beard upon him hid the details of his face, but I could tell that he was a man who had been aged by the years of his life.

"I need you to hold her still for me," his troubled voice ordered.

"Sure," I acknowledged. "What are you going to do?"

"She is having a difficult time breathing. I think she may have a collapsed lung. We can help her, but if you really want to save her, you will need to get her to a clinic," he explained as he worked. Several times, he glanced up in order to make sure that I was listening to his words.

"There is a clinic called Noah's Ark just down the road. You can take her there," he said, as he searched through a brown satchel that was slung carelessly over his shoulder.

"I know exactly what clinic you are talking about," I informed the strange man, without offering him any more details than I felt were necessary. I just kept watching him pull several medical supplies from his bag. I couldn't help but wonder why he would have those items in his possession.

"Good," he replied, motioning for me to come closer to

the deer. Gently, he placed my hands upon the doe's head and repeated, "I need you to hold her completely still for me. I need to splint her leg before we move her. We don't want to hurt her any further."

"Okay," I confidently said, agreeing to his idea. I knew exactly what procedure he was about to attempt to perform. I had helped my grandfather and Anneal many times before.

I felt terrible for the young doe. She couldn't comprehend the fact that we were trying to help her, and the worst part was the fact that she had no idea if her baby was safe or not. Her frightened eyes summoned horrible past visions to my mind. I wondered if the members of my family had been more frightened for their own lives, as they lay dying, or for those who were to survive them.

"Okay," he began, "she has an open fracture on her right front leg, so what I am going to do is splint it so that she doesn't cause more damage to it. Also, this will hopefully prevent any more debris or microorganisms from infecting the wound.

"I'm just going to slip this gauze pad between the leg and the bone, and now I'm going to place one over the top of the bone and secure them with a bandage and tape. Now, I need..."

"Excuse me," I interrupted, "but I think she is losing consciousness."

"Poor thing must be in terrible pain and so frightened," Gail thought.

"Yeah, we need to get her to the clinic so we can get a chest tube in place," he concluded. "Did you drive here?"

"Yes."

"I'm going to finish splinting the leg. Why don't you go and get your jeep ...or whatever it is you drive."

"My jeep? How did he know what I drove? Lucky guess.

Most people in these parts have a truck or jeep with four-wheel drive," she determined, but still kept a tight grasp upon the suspicion in the back of her mind.

By the time I had arrived back to help the stranger, he had already finished splinting the doe's leg and had managed to roll the doe onto a large sleeping bag that was once attached to his satchel. He was kneeling patiently next to her, while affectionately stroking her muzzle. His kind and tender personality was very evident. It was obvious he cared a great deal for the wildlife around him.

"Grab a side," he ordered, as he leapt to his feet and slung his pack carelessly over his shoulder. "We really need to hurry."

Once inside the jeep, I convinced myself to confess my familiarity with the shelter, though I still did not deem it necessary to fill him in on the entire situation. There was something perplexing about him, but at the same time I felt completely enchanted by him. His dirt-washed appearance had been the only trait keeping me from completely rendering myself to his entrancing personality.

"There is a back way in right over there," I informed him, as we recklessly rolled into the parking lot. "We can take her through those doors. The operating room is directly to the left. While you get her set up, I will find Anneal," I said, as we pulled up next to the shelter.

"She is the only doctor?" he questioned in a grunt, as we lugged the doe inside.

"No," I returned. "Anneal is not a doctor. She is working on obtaining her D.V.M. We have one other doctor who is leaving at the end of the summer. If we don't find a replacement by August, the facility will be shut down."

"Oh," he said without care, as we placed the doe on the operating table.

"I am assuming that you can find everything you need?" I asked him. "I need to find Anneal, and she needs to call Doctor Temper so that he doesn't turn us in for illegally performing operations in the clinic."

"Yes, I can find everything I need. Go find your friend quickly."

I watched the two of them work together in complete admiration. The stranger's ability to take control of the situation and turn it around from bleak to hopeful inspired an idea.

The man obviously didn't look like he had had a job in months or possibly years. His grim condition told me that he was in desperate need of assistance. The possibility of unveiling a job opportunity could change the man's future outlook.

"I'm going to go ahead and place a stomach tube in her. By the looks of her, I doubt she will be ready to feed herself anytime soon," I heard him say to Anneal. "Did you get hold of your doctor?"

"I asked Gail to call for me, so I could help you. I think she was able to reach him."

It was true. She had asked me to call him for her, but I didn't. I was more interested in what the stranger could do to save the deer. I wasn't particularly fond of Doctor Temper anyway. I was quite sure that he would be very upset with my choice in letting a strange man perform medical procedures in the shelter. Though it was against the law to allow him to operate in a facility he was not employed or licensed at, it wasn't a concern of mine. He saved the doe's life. Now the fawn would not have to know what it is like to grow up without parents, and that was a good enough reason for me.

Walking in the room, I first watched the man place the

stomach tube before making my confession. I wanted to observe every detail. Although I had never performed the surgeries myself, I knew exactly how they were done. I'd spent my whole life watching my grandfather execute them himself.

First, he measured out the length of the doe's thorax by stopping halfway down between the snout and chest. When he was certain that he had measured out the correct length of tubing, he marked it at the top and bottom with a red marker. Next, he cut the tube at the bottom on the red line that he had marked earlier. Then, he slowly and cautiously inserted the tube down the esophagus. There was little resistance, so he decided that he was all right to continue.

He leaned forward and listened to the doe's breathing in order to make sure she was not in any distress and to double-check that the tubing had been inserted correctly. If the tubing had slipped into her trachea, it would be even more difficult to take a breath than it already was for her.

When he was satisfied with her vital signs, he continued to cautiously push the tube forward. As soon as his fingers covered the red marking placed at the top of the tube, he stopped shoving forward. Finally, he puffed a small amount of air into the tube. Instantly, gastric juices began to flow through the tube. This indicated that there was a negative gravitational flow on it.

As soon as the man securely attached the tubing to the doe, I decided it was the best time to make my confession. Arrogantly, I blurted out, "I didn't call him."

"What?" he asked, as he washed his hands.

"I'm sorry?" Anneal asked in return. "You didn't call who?"

"I decided not to call Doctor Temper. It is our shelter. If anything was to go wrong, I was willing to accept the consequences of my actions. They are planning on shutting us down anyway, and our doctor is willing to leave and let it happen. What makes you think that he really cares what happens to that deer?"

"Gail, he is going to find out," Anneal commented.

"Oh, really? It isn't like we can hide the deer," I sarcastically remarked.

"He will call the state on us and on this kind man."

"Probably. There is nothing we can do anyway. You are a year away from getting your veterinarian's doctorate, and we have nobody to take over."

"We will find somebody," she countered with hope.

"Maybe we already have," I replied, staring at the stranger. The man was leaning against the sink and staring at the floor before him. I could tell that he was in deep thought, and he wasn't listening to our words.

"Don't bring me into this," he commented, when he realized we were staring impatiently at him. He quickly gathered his things when the reality of the situation came back to him.

"Oh, come on!" I shouted. "You are a veterinarian, right? Are you licensed?"

"Yes, but I'm not going back to working at a vet."

"Why not? It is a shelter. It isn't a vet," Anneal remarked.

"Forget it, and your doctor can't report me for operating on the deer without his permission if he doesn't have my name," he said, walking out the door of the operating room in a hurry.

"Hey, it is our facility, and I won't report you!" I called after him.

But the stranger left the shelter without glancing back. He wasn't interested in their invitation at the time. He was a man in search of another path to follow home.

"I really wish I knew his name," I said with disappointment.

"Why didn't you ask him?"

"It never really came up," I stated. "He was very devoted to that deer."

"He was kind of weird-looking, anyway. Not a very clean-cut guy, but he sure knew what he was doing. Kind of a weird situation," Anneal stated. "I mean, if he doesn't work at a vet, why did he have all those medical supplies with him?"

"Yes, he sure was good with his hands," I commented, but did not respond to her remarks about my stranger's appearance. "I wonder what else he is good with," I joked.

"Eww," she chuckled. "He wasn't that cute. He needs to shave and cut his hair. His clothes were awfully scraggly. I mean his jeans were completely torn, and his pocket was falling off his shirt."

"I hardly noticed his clothes. At least he smelled good," I observed. "He can't be that bad off."

"Right," she remarked, and changed the subject by asking, "So, how are you doing?"

Rolling my eyes, I answered, "Not bad."

"Are you sure? I talked to Damien before you showed up with that deer, and he said that you completely blew up in front of the kids."

"Oh yeah, but he had nothing to do or say about that situation," I replied. "It is always my fault."

"Gail, if you need some time to get away and think, you should just go. Don't worry about how somebody else is taking it."

"Well, then why do you care about how I am taking it? You go and grieve in your own way and leave me to my grievance," I crudely remarked with an ill temper.

"Gail, I didn't mean anything by what I said. I..."

"Is she going to make it?" I asked, changing the subject. I didn't want to start a fight with my best friend again. I certainly did not want her running home and speaking to my brother about it, either.

"If she makes it through the night, I give her a fifty-percent chance."

"That is it?" I asked in shock. "Her daughter cannot live without her. She has to live. That baby is probably frightened without her. It isn't right. She needs to teach her daughter how to survive!"

"Gail! Calm down!" Anneal screamed. "Who are you talking about here, anyway?"

"Just make sure she lives," I said, and without warning turned and stormed out of the room.

On her way out of the building, Gail grabbed the knob so forcefully that when she swung open the door, her hand was smashed between it and the brick wall! Shaking her hand violently back and forth, she glanced quickly at the location of the throbbing pain. The only identifiable mark her eyes captured was the old scar tissue from an early childhood accident. In seeing it, the bitterness trapped inside her heart only deepened.

Chapter Six

A cold, lonely evening of regret infiltrated the old colonial home. The cold night was filled with the bitter memories of the past. I couldn't escape the ghosts living within me. Inside my heart, I felt abandoned and betrayed by the souls of the loved ones I hardly knew. There wasn't any place to hide. No matter where I looked or tried to hide, their apparitions danced around my perishing body. The smell of rotting flesh filled the air and spread its disease within me. My blood boiled with fear as my heart began to pound against my aching chest. It felt as though my heart would burst from its ribbed cage at any moment. I once again tried to bury my head inside a familiar sanctuary, but beneath the sheltering quilt on the couch, the images still found a way to hunt me down.

"Go away!" I screamed in horror. "Just go away!"

Ring! Ring! sounded the ear-piercing phone.

"Just shut up!" I shrieked, and with all my fury, I ripped the phone from the wall and threw it forcibly into the flaming fire before me. I watched it scatter across the bare, hardwood floor, as it shattered against the red brick of the fireplace. "Why is this happening? What kind of God are you? You took everything from me, everything! Why can't you just help me? Do something great for once! Why..." I cried, as I sank upon the floor beneath me.

Like a child, she curled into a ball and wept until she fell fast asleep.

"Gail! Gail, wake up!" *called a voice in the distance.*

"Huh?" *she asked in delirium.*

"Gail, it is me, Grandma."

"Grandma," *she questioned,* "what are you doing here?"

"What do you mean? I live here now. I tried to call you, but nobody answered the phone."

"Wait," *she said with confusion* "what do you mean that you live here now?"

"Just what I said. I want to live with the two of you. You are staying here, aren't you?"

"What? No, Grandma, we went to live with Noah, remember?"

"No, no, hon. He is gone now. I want you to stay here with me," she explained, as the room opened up before them. They were not standing in the same living room where Gail had fallen asleep. They were standing in a room Gail had buried in her heart as a child.

"Oh my God!" I cried, as I awoke on the floor, surrounded by the objects I had chosen to live near.

The death of Noah had sparked an internal flame that could no longer be smothered. Even the rain falling within her heart could not douse the fire now raging in her soul. Even the fear that kept her grounded for so long had burnt and melted away. The heat of the passion would never smolder until she could find an equal balance.

Chapter Seven

Dear Damien and Anneal,
I know I have not been myself lately, but with everything that has happened recently, I feel as though I was forced to be someone that I am not. I cannot go on pretending that nothing has changed. If pretending makes you comfortable, then by all means, act as though everything is perfect in your lives. But I cannot forget about a man's smile that used to light up the room. I can't act as though I have never seen it. Every time I turn around, I expect to see him standing there, but then I realize that I'll never again see him waiting for me to return home after a long day of tireless work. Worst of all, he'll never be around to greet us with the waking sun each morning. He won't be there to make us whole again.

Even though he isn't here to help us through this, I know that he would want us to go on with our lives. I know this because he told us this while we prepared and waited for his death. I just don't think that I can go on like this, not here. I can't be here without him. The only way that I can be free once again is to start from the beginning. I feel that it is time for me to go back to the place I first died and try to be born again. It is the only way I can find myself. I must start over.

Gail

"She is going back to see <u>them</u>. I know she is."

"Maybe you should have called them in the first place, and this would not be happening."

"They abandoned us long ago, Anneal!"

"How do you know? You were just a kid, and so was she. Maybe you remember what you want to remember. Maybe you have lied so much that it has become the truth."

"<u>They</u> don't care, or <u>they</u> would have visited!"

"If they didn't care at all, why did they write your family letters once a year in response to Noah's letters? You could have shared them with the rest of your family. Noah didn't even know that they even bothered to write back."

"If you thought they were important, then you should have said something."

"Sometimes you can be a jerk, Damien! It was not my place!"

"They hate my sister!!!"

Chapter Eight

*T**he winding road that spread before Gail opened the door to endless possibilities. With each curve in the road, another line to her storybook had been written. Every bump on the black concrete served as a climax of adventure and lessons to be learned. Even though the road chosen was full of ups and downs, her creator imagined colorful sunsets at the bottom of every hill. Each sunset would eventually fade into a new beginning, leaving the darkness behind.*

She was ready to challenge any obstacle on her path, but she could not quite reach the hand of opportunity that spread wide before her. She was blind to the actions she needed to take in order to embrace the challenges of life with faith and understanding. She simply could not comprehend the meaning of her leave or why leaving the recent past behind would not solve the problems she had been facing at the time.

As I drove my life into a new chapter, the night began to

display its artistic abilities. The fireflies of the mountains spread their wings and took flight. Their angelic bodies looped and whirled messages to the sleeping world. Hundreds of thousands gathered to guide me along my way. It looked as though the heavenly stars had floated to earth in order to shine bright and guide me on my journey.

As I watched each one with gleaming eyes, abruptly, they began to silently flicker and disappear. Suddenly, I took notice that one had landed on my dashboard, but with a bright flash, it disappeared into the night. Then, quickly it reappeared one last time as if it were an aphasic warning from the world above me. Its brilliant light had illuminated the empty gas gauge of the jeep!

Feeling overwhelmed, my stomach turned. A sharp pain of fear kicked inside me until it was exhaled out. During all of the chaotic excitement earlier that day, I had completely forgotten to even check the jeep for gas!

Out of nowhere, a small, brown wooden sign flashed along the right side of my jeep. The sign was almost completely blocked by the thick brush along the berm. The pitch black of the night made it nearly impossible to read the tiny printing in a hurry. Luckily, I was able to catch the words, "gas and lodging next right, one mile."

So carefully, I searched for the lodge and hoped that I would not pass it along the way by mistake. As I rounded a steep bend in the road, a short driveway emerged from the woods on the right hand side of the road. A sharp squeal of the brakes brought the jeep to a complete halt in the middle of the road. I put the car into reverse and backed it up until I could pull safely onto the drive.

The gravel landing led forward a few feet and dissipated into a paved path. Its narrow straightway made it entirely inconceivable for one to even think about passing another car, and it was entirely impossible to imagine what lay ahead beyond the path. I wished that I had never pulled off the main road, but I persuaded myself to continue traveling forward. It would have been very difficult to turn back after that point.

When the jeep finally reached the other side of the drive, I sharply turned it left, past the edge of a gated swimming pool. There was just enough room for a vehicle to pass, but the path quickly gave way to an enormous parking lot filled with a resplendent log cabin with a four-car gas garage behind it. As impressive as the lodge seemed, only a few cars lined the entrance.

After filling up my gas tank, I pulled up next to the lodge entrance. The hidden lodge in the woods stood alone, strong and unyielding. A few travelers rushed in and out of the entrance and exit until they scattered with the wind. The beautiful lodge blended in with the woods as if it had been carved out of nature itself! Blossoms from trees and flowers laid themselves down upon the roof and cobblestone patio. When the blossoms swayed in the breeze, it gave the lodge a somber appearance in harmony.

Silky white candles radiated light from the arched windows that decorated the oak walls. The peaceful feeling perceived at first glance welcomed all visitors to step inside its walls. I was baffled by the fact that in all the years I had lived in the state of Washington, I never knew the lodge existed. Yet, in another sense, the appearance of the lodge seemed so familiar and welcoming that I felt as if I had been there before that very night.

As I stepped outside my jeep, I was greeted by the four winds rushing toward the candlelight inside. I opened the door of the entrance, and the winds from all corners followed me inside. With the closing of the doors, the winds licked at the candle flames and flicked at their burning core. Each of the flames seemed to dance and frolic with the shadows on the walls. They laughed and laughed as the winds proceeded to tickle them.

Directly across from me were two restrooms with a drinking fountain separating them. On each of the doors hung a hand painting, which revealed the gender allowed behind them. In fact, as I looked around the lobby, I noticed that all of the walls were covered in very artistic paintings. It was quite obvious that the hand that painted them stemmed from a deep and beautiful soul.

"Can I help you, miss?" sounded an old, deep voice from behind the counter. Even though his voice sounded so harsh, it was still altogether soothing.

"Um, yeah. I purchased gas, and I wouldn't mind having a room," I spoke up.

"Okay, that is twenty fifty-seven for the gas and fifty-four dollars for the room. That comes to seventy-eight thirty-five with tax," he informed, as he added the numbers with his calculator.

"Great, thank you," I said, as I reached out to pay the wrinkled-faced man. He instantly turned around to select a key from the wall and began to hand it over to me.

With the keys dangling slightly above my fingertips, he replied, "You look very familiar to me. Have we met before?"

"No, I don't think so. I haven't been out this way since I was a young child. I doubt this place even existed back then."

"You might be surprised. This place has been here since I was a young man about your age. I should know, because I opened it up. Of course, there have been some major renovations since back then. It was just a campground back then, but I have always been here, and I am quite certain that I do know you."

"I don't know," I said in frustration. I was positive that the man had never seen me before. "Maybe you saw somebody who looks like me."

"Well, no matter," he said, dropping the keys in my hand. "Just sign here, and I will show you to your room. It is just around the corner," he informed me. "It overlooks the pool," he expressed with pride. "So you know, the lobby is always open. I will always have tea and coffee made, and there are always donuts or muffins."

"Okay, thank you," I said, as I handed the man the receipt. "I think I can find the room myself," I informed him in hopes of escaping sooner.

"Okay, then," he replied. Yet, with a startle he shouted after me, "Just a minute! I do know you. You are Gail Rein!"

"Yes," I answered in annoyance. "Very good. That is what it says on the receipt."

"No, no. You used to come here with your grandparents and your parents before the accident. Of course, after the accident, your family stopped coming altogether. Good people they were, the both of them."

"You knew my parents?" I questioned in disbelief. I hardly knew my parents, but a strange man behind a counter could tell if they were good or bad.

"Oh, yes," he responded with delight, but his expression quickly turned grim. "What a horrible accident that was. Just an act of God. There wasn't anything anyone could have done for them. I'm even more sorry that you and your brother had to witness it."

"Yeah, well, I don't really remember much about it," I commented, as I tried to shove the past behind me. "I was just a little kid."

"How is your brother, though? He sure was big enough to understand."

"He is fine," I answered in short.

"I was just thinking of the time the two of you were last here," he relentlessly continued, despite my obvious short-tempered demeanor. "The two of you decided that you just had to go hiking, despite the fact that it had been raining all day long. Now back then, mind you, I just had campsites for tents and unpaved walking paths, but you had to go even though your parents and I warned you not to. By the time the two of you got back here, you were covered head to toe in mud, and I mean literally covered. Your grandparents brought you inside here...well, the lobby back then that is, but anyway, they brought you in here to clean you up in the sinks of the restrooms. Funniest thing I had ever seen. So the..."

"Oh my God," I sounded, as the old man kept rambling on about his past memory. His story was beginning to sound very familiar. "I do remember this place!" I said ecstatically. "The restrooms were right over there. It was the only place that had any shower stalls, but the showers weren't working back then."

"That is right," he agreed.

"I remember, because right after we were cleaned up, Damien fell back into the mud we had tracked inside. He busted his lip open, and you brought him some towels and ice. I kept trying to thank you, but I couldn't say your name!" I recollected joyously.

"Yes, you kept calling me Zekirah, and I kept trying to correct you."

"Yeah, I remember that."

"How about my name? Do you remember it?"

"Yes, it is Zachariah Nobals."

"Yes, you do remember," he answered warmly. "It has been so long. At times I wondered how you and your family were doing."

"Ah well," I began, as I searched for the right words, "we are surviving the best we can."

"How about Noah? How is he doing? I know he was struck pretty hard by the accident. He even blamed himself."

"A lot of people blamed him and still do."

"He doesn't believe it was his fault still, does he?"

"I'm not sure he ever really did blame himself. I think he just wished there was more he could have done to help them."

"Well, he saved the two of you, and that should count for something. Tell the old man to come up and see me."

Sighing, I innocently stared into Zachariah's eyes as if I were searching for the right words to say, but sadly I found nothing in the way of comfort. So, humbly I stuttered out the only words I could find in my heart. "Um, Noah...he...ah, he recently passed away. I'm...actually on my way up to inform my other grandparents about his passing."

"Oh, well, my goodness. He was only a few years younger than me. Do you mind me asking what happened?"

"Ah, it was cancer, actually."

"Oh, no. What kind of cancer did he have?"

"It was esophageal cancer," I informed him, and added, "but he lived a good life. He was eighty. Disease or not, a lot of people never have the chance to live that long."

"Couldn't they do anything for him? Didn't he have early symptoms?"

"I don't know. I don't really want to talk about it."

"Well, I suppose it was his time to go, right?"

"Sure, whatever," I responded with regretful hostility. "I'm sorry. I'm a little tired, and I'm trying to figure out how to cope with everything while everyone keeps asking me all these questions. I've been a little annoyed lately."

"It is in good reason, Gail. Healing takes time."

"Healing takes time, but life offers none," I sharply replied. "Good night."

"Life offers all the time you need to complete it," he called after my fleeing body. "Good night, Gail," he continued, as I rushed outside through the main lodge entrance.

Locating the room was not terribly difficult. It stood exactly where Zachariah had described, overlooking a gorgeous in-ground swimming pool. On the west side of the pool, a small but intricately designed cascade sloped and formed an exquisitely gentle rolling waterfall.

On the opposite side of the pool, the words "deep end" vividly made an appearance. I found it interesting that the most dangerous end of the pool happened to be located near the most unsafe area in the parking lot. There seemed to be a theme, and I didn't like the superstitious idea behind it.

"Soothing, isn't it?" sounded a familiar voice from behind me.

Startled and unable to place a face with the voice, I quickly whirled around in order to discover who possessed the alarming voice. Completely caught off guard, I could not find any words to express my opinion.

"Are you following me?" the stranger speculated.

"What? No...I..."

"Relax," he ordered. "I was kidding."

"Oh," I responded with relief. "Um, so what are you doing here?"

"Just passing through. You?"

"Same here," I answered. "Where are you headed?"

"Toward White Salmon. How about you?"

"Actually, in the opposite direction. I am on the way to

Clearwater."

"Oh, it is beautiful there. Do you have family there?"

"Yes, in a way they are considered family."

"Oh, one of those kinds of family. I can relate," he chuckled. "So, how is the deer?"

"Well, she was doing okay the last time I heard."

"Good," he commented. "Well, I should let you get to your room."

"Oh, right. You would probably like to get to yours also."

"No, not really. I just came from there. I was a little bored."

"Oh," I responded thoughtfully. "Well, maybe after I get settled, we can get together to talk," I boldly suggested. Suddenly I felt my heart skip a beat and leap into my throat. Quickly, I choked it back down and felt my stomach churn in surprise.

"Ah, sure," was all he managed to say. I could feel the heat from his blushing cheeks radiate in my direction.

"Okay, then."

"Yes, sounds good."

"Then I'll go and meet you at your room."

"My room."

"Yes," I agreed, and turned to leave before I realized that I didn't know where his room was located. "Oh, ah...your room is where?"

"One-oh-six," he replied.

"Really? That is easy to remember. Mine is one-oh-five. We are next door to each other. So, okay. I'll see you."

"Yes," he agreed. "Gail, right?" he asked, as he searched for a seat next to the pool, but by mistake, he leaned upon the handle of the chair and nearly tipped it over. He quickly regained control of his balance by sitting upon the seat before he had completely fallen to the ground.

"Yes, and I'm sorry, but I don't think that I ever caught your name," I responded with embarrassment.

"I don't think I ever said it," he reported, as if he were trying to make me feel better. "It is Caden."

"Caden? I like that. You don't hear it that often," I told him with a smile before opening the door to my room. He just grinned with acknowledgment and stared at my beaming face until the door closed behind me.

Chapter Nine

"Sorry I took so long," I stated to Caden. He had found a seat near the deep end of the pool and had become entranced by its soothing sound.

"That's all right. I actually enjoyed sitting out here near the pool," he said, as he turned around to face me. "Wow!" he exclaimed. "You look, um, beautiful."

Gail's blushing skin beamed brilliantly in the glistering glow cast by the full moon above the two of them. Her usual pulled-back hair had been let down in order to flap in the slight breeze surrounding them. It seemed to wave and call out for Caden's attention. Even her strikingly slender body seemed to catch the lonely eyes of his dispirited soul. Though she had not purposely dressed with intentions of attracting him, her instinctive responses took control subconsciously.

"Oh," I stammered, "Wow! Thank you." I was positive that my face was bright red. There was something that positively attracted me toward him that I couldn't explain. I hoped that my appearance and behavior weren't too bold. "Um, so have you always been a veterinarian?"

"No, not always," Caden shyly answered, before promptly changing the subject. He didn't come across as a man interested in revealing any vulnerable information. "What is it that you do? You don't work at the vet, so you what? Just travel around rescuing creatures in need of your assistance?"

"No," I smirked. "That actually sounds more like you. I actually," I began to say, but was caught off guard by an eerie sound in the distance. "What is that?" I asked, as the distracting sound seemed to be coming closer.

"I think it is coming from the driveway. It sounds like brakes."

"I think it is brakes!" I screamed, as the frightening noise inevitably approached closer and closer.

"Look out!" Caden warned, as the front cab of a passenger truck lunged toward the pool's fence. Just before striking the fence head on, the truck slammed on its brakes once more and cut the wheel sharply to the left. The back of its bed came smashing directly into the fence! The two of us stumbled backwards until we slipped into the water of the pool! Instantly, my body was overcome with the sharp burning sting of fire. It felt as though my body had been hurled upon a bed of concrete. I forced myself to hold my breath and not scream out in excruciating pain.

In moments, the diminishing pain was replaced by an exhilaration of warmth. My yielding skin accepted the heat's tender touch as I sank deeper into the water's clutch. Its pacifying heat cradled my surrendering body within its waves. My deceived mind wanted to sink forever into its depths and remain for an eternity.

Suddenly, my body was shaken awake by the tightening

of my screaming lungs. My eyes jerked themselves open and searched for an escape route, but they were blinded from above by a bright flash of light. My lungs fought to maintain control, but with each passing second, they collapsed closer to death.

Then, there above me, the light dimmed, and my path to freedom appeared. Kicking and punching at the water, my body struggled to survive. With each forward stroke, my lungs filled with relief, but still the end of my journey seemed so far away. Each time I thought the surface was near, it disappeared from sight. It was as though my body kept swimming forward, and the water kept getting deeper! With one last burst of energy, I lunged toward the surface. Just as I broke through and gasped for breath, my body was yanked back beneath the surface! Choking for air, my lungs cried out in pain, but something kept pulling me farther and farther below! Whirling around rapidly to face my captor, I was greeted by the frightened eyes of Caden. His dying body called out for help!

Quickly extending my hand farther below the surface, I frantically searched for something to grasp. Suddenly, I felt the grip of his hand clinging to my waist. With all of my might, I yanked him closer to my chest. Breaking the surface of the pool, we choked oxygen back into our lungs.

"There they are!" I heard voices shouting from all around. My eyes were blinded by the lights shining upon us.

"I can't swim!" Caden cried aloud to me.

"I've got you," I assured him. "I won't let you go."

And she meant it. She would have died saving him if there wasn't another way. She would not stand by and let another innocent victim die before her eyes.

"Gail! Gail! Swim to me," I heard Zachariah calling from somewhere around us. My blurred and watery eyes tried to focus on him as I swam toward the side of the pool. "Are you guys all right?" his worried voice questioned, as he helped us out of the pool. Our shivering bodies were greeted by several strangers offering to help.

"I'm so sorry," cried a red-eyed man. His stumbling feet wobbled all over the pool deck as he helped the others pull Caden and me off of the cold ground.

"You're drunk!" a woman shouted. "No wonder you ran into the pool!"

"The fence!" he corrected. "There is a difference! The driveway is so narrow that I couldn't see a thing."

"You could have killed them!" the man next to the shouting woman concluded. "The parking lot may be a death trap, but a sober man could pilot his way through it."

"I'm calling the police!" Zachariah shouted in return.

"No!" the shivering Caden urged. "We are just fine. Please, just give the man a room to sleep it off."

"He nearly killed you!" Zachariah argued.

"I know that, but if the cops come here, we will be up all night filling out a report, and I just want to go inside to put on some dry clothes. Everyone needs a second chance," Caden commented.

Nodding as if there were a secret between the two of them, Zachariah caved at Caden's words. "Do you feel the same?" he asked me.

Shocked and surprised by Caden's mercy, I just agreed to free the man from his trials. I didn't know what else to say. I didn't want to come across as an unforgiving person. "Yes, that's fine. We are alive, and I just want to go inside and take a warm bath."

"Oh, thank you," the drunken man clamored. "You are too kind. I'm very sorry. So sorry." he continued to shout, as Caden led me away from the scene of the accident. "I'm going to quit drinking! Not tonight, but tomorrow morning! That is a promise!"

"Personally, sir, I would have sent you to jail!" I heard the other strange man say to the drunken driver as I searched for my room key in my saturated jean pocket. The argument seemed to relentlessly continue back and forth.

"I can't find the key," I said aloud to Caden with annoyance. "I'm freezing, and I just want to get inside."

"It's okay," he comforted. "I have mine right here," he said, opening the door to his room. "We can dry off and look for yours later."

"Okay," I nodded. "Why are they arguing with that drunken idiot anyway?" I asked furiously, as Caden and I scrambled through the door of his room. "They weren't even involved in the accident. Why do some people have to stick their nose into everyone else's business, like they have a right to interfere and feel the same way as the party involved does?"

"Wow!" Caden offered as answer. "We aren't just talking about the accident here, are we?"

Throwing my arms up in the air, I said, "Oh, forget it. I just need some sleep."

Rushing into the bathroom, Caden said, "Let me get you a towel. You can dry off and change in the bathroom if you want. I'm okay out here," he stated, as he handed me a couple of red towels. "When I'm done changing, I'll go get us some tea or coffee or something."

"Hot tea sounds good, thanks."

Holding out his hands as if he were guiding me to the bathroom, he remarked, "It is all yours."

Shuffling my feet with embarrassment, I finally reminded Caden, "I don't have any clothes to change into."

"Oh, right," he remembered, and began to rummage

through his old dingy satchel. "You can just wear this flannel until I get back. I'll just get another key from Zachariah while I'm out," he suggested, as he held a blue and green flannel up in front of me.

"Okay. Thanks," I replied. "I don't suppose you happen to have a pair of pink panties in there?"

"No," he chuckled, "but would you settle for a pair of pink boxers? They used to be white, but a friend of mine has a little trouble with his vision and washed them with a red shirt."

"Right," I smiled.

"By the way, thanks."

"For what?"

"For saving my life."

Chapter Ten

"Phew," I said, stepping out of the shower. My body was instantly attacked by hot steam. So, instinctively, I partially opened the door and wiped off the mirror before dressing. My overheated body shuddered at the thought of buttoning the heavy flannel, so I began to brush and dry my hair with the shirt dangling from my shoulders. The lodge hair dryer was very loud and extremely inefficient for my long brown hair. It seemed as though I had been attempting to dry it for an eternity.

"Hey, I got your key and brought you some tea, but ...Oh!" Caden gasped. "I'm sorry.

I heard the dryer and thought you were covered," he explained, with his head bowed to the ground, yet his eyes kept trying to sneak another peek.

"It's okay," I remarked, while pulling the shirt tightly around my shoulders. "It was my fault that the door was open."

Despite the intensity in the room, Gail never felt the discomfort of embarrassment. She was quite pleased by his reaction to her body. More than anything, she felt relief in the fact that Caden attempted to sneak another glance.

Gazing intensely at me, he began to finish his earlier statement but this time with care and tenderness in his voice. "I wasn't sure which kind of tea you wanted, so I brought back several different kinds. They are out here on the counter when you are ready."

"Thank you," I replied. "That was very kind of you. I'll just button up and be right out."

"Okay," he nodded. "Just shout if you need any help. The buttons on that shirt can be pretty tricky," he commented and closed the door behind him.

Laughing to myself as Caden walked away, I realized that I was not embarrassed by knowing that he had seen my naked body. An innocent feeling of warmth filled my body each time I recalled the bashful yet extremely audacious expression plastered upon his face when he walked in on me. His flattering confidence appealed significantly to my emotional senses. Discovering who he was inside began to be the only objective careening throughout my aroused mind.

"Are you still cold?" I asked him, as I walked out of the bathroom. I found him sipping his tea while sitting on a chair before the fireplace. The teacup still rattled in his hand.

"A little," he admitted with honesty. "But the shaking might be from wondering what you are thinking about me, since I walked in on you."

"I'm not thinking anything. It was an accident."

"I should have knocked before opening the door, though. I'm sorry," he apologized again.

"Don't worry about it," I told him. "I should probably go

to my room and find some actual clothes."

"No," he quickly interjected. "I mean, at least have some tea. I got it just for you," he pointed out smoothly.

"Okay," I nodded, and took a seat on the bed across from him. I positioned myself near the headboard with a pillow draped across my lap.

"What kind would you like?" he asked, while holding the tea up and smiling sweetly at me. I was sure he was laughing at the pillow. "Ah, there is regular, cinnamon apple, orange spice, and peach."

"Peach sounds good," I answered with a smile, careful not to disturb the pillow on my lap.

With a chuckle he said, "You can go change if you are uncomfortable. I just want to make sure that you are going to come back."

"Actually, I think I will be okay," I said.

"Well, it won't be any fun if you are going to sit so stiffly all night," he joked, handing me the cup of tea.

"Hey, you're not the one sitting around in clothes that belong to someone you hardly know. Not to mention, there is a hole in these boxers, and it is quite drafty in here," I reasoned.

Bellowing with laughter, he pointed out, "The hole is there for easy access, sweetheart. And I am not that much of a stranger. Ask me anything you want, and I might give you an answer."

"You might give me an answer, huh?"

"Sure," he said, sitting back in his chair and throwing his legs upon the foot of the bed.

"Okay, there is something I am wondering about. Why did you let that man go when he nearly killed you?"

"Everyone deserves a second chance," he repeated.

"Yes, but what if he does it again? Maybe some jail time

would do him good."

"The man was aware of what he did. He wasn't that wasted. I think the parking lot played a role in the accident. Zachariah has been talking about widening it for a while. Maybe this incident will persuade him to take action. Things happen for a reason."

"Are you close to Zachariah?" I asked. "The two of you seemed to have a connection back there."

"He offers me a place stay in exchange for some work of mine."

"So what is it you do?"

"I paint," he remarked simply.

"Oh, did you paint those pictures in the lobby?"

"Yes, I painted most of the pictures and most of these rooms for him."

"Oh, wow! Every one of the paintings is beautiful. You're very talented with your hands," I teased.

"Thank you very much. I can do many things with them," he informed me.

"Right," I chuckled. "Do you think that you could shave with them? Or cut your hair?" I asked, imitating a hand shaving an imaginary beard on my face.

"Don't pick on my beard and hair. They took a long time to grow."

"But you can't even see your face," I told him. "I want to see the face of the man I saved. Aren't I supposed to be responsible for you now? How am I supposed to protect you if I can't recognize you?"

"Well, what would you do for me if you were responsible for me?" he asked, while gazing into my eyes.

"Shave your beard, and you'll see," I flirted.

"Oh, I see how it is. Maybe you should give me a taste of what you are going to do to me?"

"Come on. What are you hiding?" I cautiously investigated. "Why are you hiding your face from the world? What could be so horrifying about you?" I inquired, sliding closer to him, the pillow still laced to my lap.

"You might be surprised," he commented, with sadness locked within his gruff voice.

"There are a lot of things that I'm not proud of in my life, too, but I don't hide my face from the world," I explained, while brushing my hand across his cheek.

For a moment he closed his eyes and pushed my hand closer to his face. Then, without warning, he accused, "No, you just run away."

Pulling my hand from his cheek, I confessed, "Yeah, I run away. It is easier than dealing with the pain."

"Sometimes I run, too," he whispered in my ear as he proceeded closer to my lips. With his lips ever so lightly brushing mine, he quietly asked, "Would you like to see what I hide from the world?"

Understanding life and learning to cope with the challenges dealt within a lifetime are the most crucial pieces of life's puzzle to solve. Without deciphering the riddle of your life, you can never develop a strong framework to continue adding pieces to your life's puzzle; an image of who you are can never begin. In other words, man cannot find his true identity without first discovering life.

When man finally understands his true identity, it is amazing how everything that once defined him begins to fade from his life. The little things that once meant the world to him gradually melt away until they are mere memories in the back of his mind.

"Everything and everyone I have ever loved in my life have gone away," Caden explained to me as I sat propped upon the bathroom countertop in the bathroom. "I blame myself for the death of my wife and daughter. After the accident, I was left with horrific scars across my face. Every time I looked into the mirror, I judged myself with the burden of their death, so I hid my face, not from the world. I could not bear the pain of death any longer," he said, in a confession that melted both his heart and mine. The pain of his agony was the same burden I carried since I was a child.

Choking back my tears, I asked, "What happened to them? What is it that you blame yourself for?"

"There is only one other person I have told about this," he remarked.

"Then why did you decide to tell me?"

"Because I trust you inexplicably. Everything that you do comes from your heart. Even the way you were willing to save that deer. Though you were hurting badly, you still found the courage to help another living creature.

"And when you saved my life tonight, you were well on your way to death yourself. You may not think that you are an amazing person, but I think you have one of the most beautiful souls ever created," Caden informed me, with pure honesty that stemmed from deep within his soul. I could tell his heart could not tell a lie. It only yearned to feel whole once again.

"Caden, that is the most beautiful thing that anyone has ever said to me. Most people think that I only think of myself, because of the things I say."

"Hasn't anyone ever told you that it isn't what you say but what you do? Most people are afraid of the truth. They lie to themselves for so long that they begin to believe in the lie. It is only when the lie is confessed that the truth is revealed."

"So, how do you feel about your life? Do you feel that your life is a lie?"

"Not until I met you. Which is why I need you to remove the lie."

"You want me to unmask the wrongly accused? You want me to shave your beard and trim your hair, so that you can face the villain you believe yourself to be?"

"No, I want you to unmask the villain so that I can do the time for the crime I committed."

"I'll remove the beard, but if I do, you have to explain to me the crime that you have wrongly condemned yourself with."

Heavily sighing, with tears in his eyes, he began his confession. "I was driving late one night on the old mountain pass outside this lodge. I glanced away from the road for only a minute to watch my wife and daughter sleep. When I looked back toward the road, I saw a deer standing in the middle of it. I swerved to miss it, and we were struck by a truck on the passenger side of our car. Since he was going down and we were going up, he hit us with such a force that our car flipped several times.

"I wasn't buckled in, so I flew out of the car through the driver's side window and slid several feet before blacking out. My wife and daughter were still in the car when the vehicle struck the side of the mountain.

"The doctor said that they probably died instantly, and since they were sleeping, they probably never knew what happened. All I can think about is how they might still be alive if I hadn't swerved to miss that deer. I was so worried about saving that deer that I never thought about the consequences."

"Caden," I said, spreading shaving cream across his freshly trimmed beard. I still didn't notice anything unusual about his facial features. "I'm really sorry about the accident, but you can't blame yourself for the deer being there. You made a split-second decision, and there are so many curves on that mountain pass, there is no way you could have predicted that a truck would come barreling around one. Most people would have reacted the same way."

"But it didn't happen to 'most people.' It happened to me, which is why I can't help you with the shelter."

"What do you mean?"

"After their death, I took off, and I couldn't stand the thought of placing animal life over a human's life, which is why I am not a veterinarian anymore.

"Then, after we saved the deer together, we met up here and were nearly killed by a truck. It keeps happening over and over again."

"We were nearly killed by a drunk driver, who was driving a truck. And again I stress nearly. We are still alive. You can't believe your whole life is defined by one event. If you do, you'll never move forward. You will just keep experiencing the same thing over and over, because that is all you can think about," I pointed out.

Gail was very good at solving a problem that didn't belong to her, but she was blind to her own advice.

"I understand that now. After tonight, I realized that I didn't want to die as a man living in the past. When it is my time to go, I want to be defined as a man who knew who he was and where he came from."

"I think we all identify with the past. It tends to makes us into who we are."

"Someday I hope that man will see that we are defined by what we do," Caden declared.

"And that is why you feel you are a murderer?" I asked. "Because we are defined by what we do?"

"I know it happened in the past, but I can't escape it. I want to move forward, but I am afraid that I will be haunted by the event for an eternity."

"I guess you just have to try to move past it and figure out why you survived the accident. I'm sure it will always be a part of you, but it doesn't define you as a person. You never meant to hurt anyone. You have to believe that you are more than that," I keenly perceived.

"How do I escape this?" he asked, as he pointed to the scars on his face.

"Oh," I stated when I saw the scars of his past. "I don't know," I confessed. "I think those who are blinded by the soul's truth will define you by them, but I think it gives you character. I wouldn't have you any other way. Without them, you wouldn't be you. I wouldn't know who you are."

"I was so terrified that you would be turned off by the scars."

At first glance, the pain trapped inside his scar caused his features to look angrier than the disfigured remnants actually appeared. The scar ran across the right side of his cheek and left its impression behind the farther the eye looked back. The ugly old wound traveled from above and below his cheekbone, back to the start of his ear, and halfway down his neck. The skin seemed to be torn right from his flesh!

Timidly, I asked, "Can I touch it?"

"It doesn't hurt anymore," he reassured.

"Yes it does. Only in a different way," I commented, acknowledging his pain.

Tenderly, as if pretending to come across as brave, I traced the scar from the length of his neck and back to the side of his cheek. It was rough but, at the same time, completely smoothed over. I was unsure of how to react, and I'm quite positive to this day that I made a disgusted scowl across the brow of my face. It wasn't intentional but a natural reaction to something new and misunderstood.

Hurt by my reaction, his deep brown eyes quickly turned from mine. His wavy black hair fell to his face and partially covered his mark of embarrassment. His strong, shaking hand brushed the hair back out of his eye and collapsed silently next to his side. Quietly, he turned and left the room to hide and sulk alone in his chair next to the fireplace.

It was something new to him. It was something he would have to grow to like. A piece of him was gone. A piece of his identity had been lost forever.

<u>*Diary: Born anew*</u>

2 June, 03

I've walked dusty paths covered by unclean roads. My eyes have seen bitter days wrapped in cold nights, but I have awakened to days born of a new sun. My heart has searched for answers in life's trial but has failed to obey the final verdict. I've traveled alone on my journeys and found myself wanting.

In the light of a new experience, I have found hope in the shade of the morning's shadow that lingers near my soul. Together, my new hope and I will find the strength it takes to discover the wisdom we need to set our spirits free.

Chapter Eleven

Buckets of rain raced off the wooden roof and poured toward the pool. The once graceful cascade had transformed into a "Little Niagara," which crashed into the watery depths beneath it. The already gray sky dimmed until its light gloomed over the day. Not a sound or a creature attempted to venture out into the day's night. Only those who hid their souls from the light of the day could have survived, shadowed beneath the gray clouds of desolation.

"C'mon!" I shouted, after pounding on the door to Caden's room for several minutes. The striking rain had saturated my clothes all the way through and rolled off of my cringing skin. My skin was beginning to shake from the cold.

"You aren't going to find him there!" an old voice finally shouted over the rain.

Turning around to face Zachariah, I yelled, "What?!"

"He left earlier this morning," he replied, confirming my

suspicion. "Go inside!" he ordered, when the door that had once sheltered Caden was reopened. "He asked me not to tell you where he went, but I figured I'd better say something to you so that you would get out of this rain.

You are one stubborn girl, like your mama was. I thought that you were going to beat that door down."

"Why can't you tell me where he went?" I asked in an angry tone. The idea of Caden not wanting to see me again upset me greatly. I never meant to hurt him.

"I don't know what transpired between the two of you. I just know what he told me. He seemed troubled about something."

"I think I hurt his feelings," I confirmed with guilt.

"No, he was troubled before you came. If anything, you helped to save him a bit." He smiled with admiration. It was the kind of smile that a father gives his child the day they are born. "I noticed he shaved this morning," the old man added, his bright blue eyes still shining bright.

"He showed me the scar from his accident."

"A tragic accident. It happened right outside the lodge. I'm the one who called for help. He just can't seem to take his mind off of it. He comes back here now and then after visiting their graves. I let him stay in exchange for his talents."

"You buy paintings from him, right?"

"Yes," he said, eyes gleaming like a proud parent. "I think there is a painting that you should take a look at."

"A painting?" I sounded.

"I don't want to see a painting. I want to find Caden," Gail selfishly thought to herself.

He led the way into the main lobby and stopped when he reached the back wall. Then, he pointed to the largest painting in the building and hinted that I should pay close attention to its detail.

At first, all I saw in the picture was the back of a man, whose body was barely visible to the eye. After a closer look, I noticed there were several clues that could help lead me to Caden's location. The painting showed evidence that the man traveled alone on a highway. He was surrounded by mountains to the left, valleys to the right, and semi-trucks from the front and behind. The highway seemed to travel on forever, but I just couldn't place the road.

"How am I supposed to figure out which road he is on?" I pleaded with Zachariah.

"Tell me what you think about the painting. An artist will use everything around the environment to express himself."

"But..."

"Look at it carefully."

"Alright," I stubbornly agreed. "The man is definitely Caden, because he is alone and you can't see his face."

"Don't tell me what you know about Caden. Tell me about the painting."

"Ahh," I groaned in frustration. "The hiker seems alone. He doesn't want the rest of the world to see him, which is why his back is blurred to the viewer. He focuses on the highway, because the mountains and trees are blurry. His attention remains focused on the road, because the trucks are clear and visible. But I still don't see where he is going."

"You called him a hiker. Why?" Zachariah questioned.

"Because he looks like he is going to get aboard one of those trucks. The one traveling the same direction as him looks like it is going slower than the other one, because it is in better focus than the rest."

"Look at the truck going the other way. Look at the detail."

"Oh!" I sounded with amazement. The minuscule detail

could easily be missed. "The rearview mirror on the smaller truck has the reflection of the route in it, but it isn't backward. He can't forget about them. He can't turn from the past. He knows he'll be back. But why does he ride in the same type of trucks that his family was killed by?"

"Ironic, huh?"

"I'm going to find him. I can't just let him go," I told Zachariah. "He must be headed southwest."

"How did you know?"

"Because the mountains would be on the other side if he were going east. Plus, he told me that he was headed toward White Salmon. I just didn't know what road he took to get there. There are so many to choose from," I pointed out

"Yes, there are. Are you sure you want to choose this one?"

"I'm positive," I assured him with honesty, and turned to leave. I was in such a hurry to find Caden that I never gave Zachariah the opportunity to finish his thoughts.

"Gail!" Zachariah shouted to me, as I walked out the door.

"Yes?" I called to him, as I stuck my head back through the doorway. My legs were left waiting impatiently outside. I hoped Zachariah could not hear them thumping anxiously against the concrete walkway.

"When you find him," he began, "don't forget who you are."

"Excuse me?" I asked him. I was stunned by his statement. I could feel a cold chill race throughout my body. My mind seemed to block out everything else in existence and focus entirely on Zachariah.

"Don't forget what you started out to do," he sternly reminded, his eyebrows narrowed for more emphasis.

"Okay," I nodded, as my mind snapped itself awake in

order to allow my body to respond to the environment around it. The portion of my body that was still outside of the lodge was overcome by the power of the rain's torrent and wind. I quickly gathered my senses and exited the lodge. The copious rain made it difficult to see clearly. It was a struggle to just reach my jeep.

Once inside the jeep, my hand wanted to turn the engine over, but I couldn't escape the thoughts of Zachariah's words. And he was right. I was looking for any excuse not to finish what I had started out to do. I was certain that I wanted to follow the road Caden had chosen, even though it was in the exact opposite direction of the original path I had selected to conquer. I just kept hoping that somehow Caden and I would find a route that would lead both of us in the same direction we had primarily intended to travel.

The descending rain poured constantly upon the pane of the window, washing away any guilt and shame still entrapped in my heart. As if I were Caden's savior, I'd only hoped that I could reach him in time to stop him from making the mistake of his life. I wanted him to know that he no longer needed to hide his face from the world. If I had lost him along that lonely highway in the rain, it might have been my last chance to help him realize how special he was to me and to the rest of the world. I had to prove to him that it wasn't his fault that his family died in that car accident.

So I pulled out of the parking lot and focused my concentration on rescuing Caden. And yet, my mind gave up so easily. After only 20 minutes of relentless searching, I had given up all hope of finding him. I knew he couldn't have gotten far on foot in the weather that day. The road was barely visible to a driver. A hiker would have a difficult time seeing, as well as keeping warm in the flooding waters falling upon him. His only chance was finding help or shelter. If

Caden had found his shelter and protection from anyone, I would be too late to stop him from leaving. I was positive I had lost him forever.

"Sometimes, when all things seem impossible, it is then when we realize how possible things really can be. It is then we find the faith to follow our heart."

Gail suddenly remembered her grandfather saying this to Damien and her when they were young children. It was long ago, but she still remembered as if it were yesterday.

"Grandpa, this is impossible. We are never going to find it," Damien had whined to his grandfather during a treasure hunt he had prepared for them. It was Easter Sunday, and they were searching for the trail the Easter Bunny had left behind. Only it wasn't just a gift they were about to receive, it was a lesson about life.

"Just search through the trees and along the path. Don't be fooled by the forest. Just look beyond it for the clues that will lead you to your treasure."

"But Grandpa, other parents just give their children their gifts," Gail complained.

"If everything you were given was just handed to you by your mother, your father, or even your grandmother or me, then you would never understand what life truly meant."

"What does it mean?" Gail asked him.

"That is the right question to ask but the wrong time for an answer."

"Just look through the rain," I told myself. "Look around and you will see," I said doubtfully, as I wiped the fog from the windowpane. My face had been pressed nearly up against the glass while I hunted for my treasure.

"Oh my God!" I shouted, when I could finally see through the pouring rain. It seemed to surround me from all angles. "I can't believe it," I said, astonished by a mysterious figure in the distance who seemed to be hitching a ride in a dirty white semi-truck.

Blaring the jeep's horn, I raced toward the finish line. I was not about to let anyone steal the lost treasure I had been searching to find. Swerving onto the berm on the opposite side of the truck, I slammed on my brakes until the jeep came to a skidding halt next to Caden. He had been standing on the rail of the truck just outside of the door. His eyes were searching for the sound of the approaching car.

"What are you doing?" he furiously asked when I opened the door to my jeep.

"Following you," I stated, remembering the second time we had met at the lodge's pool.

"Why? Zachariah wasn't supposed to tell you where I was going," he said argumentatively, his saturated body shivering in the cold. His wet and matted hair drooped across the brow of his face. It helpfully covered up any grimace upon his face.

"He didn't tell me where you went, but that is why I am here."

"What? Why?" he asked with frustration, but not with me. He kept trying to wipe the rain from his eyes, but he couldn't find a dry spot on his dingy green coat. "Come inside," he motioned, climbing aboard the truck.

"Is the girl coming, too?" asked the truck driver.

"No, um, Ed this is Gail. Gail, Ed."

"Nice to meet you," he replied. "Caden and I go way back. We were involved in an accident together. This is the first time I have seen him without his beard since that day."

"An accident?" I questioned in shock.

"Yes," Ed confirmed.

"He was the truck driver," Caden announced.

"You're hitching a ride from the guy..."

Cupping his hand over my mouth, as if he didn't want to hear the truth, and shaking his head 'yes,' he answered my question without using any words. For a man who was torn apart by the death of his wife and daughter, he certainly had a way of expressing the blame he carried for himself.

"How did you find me?" he finally asked.

"I saw your painting of the mountain pass, and it led me here."

"Why did you come?"

"Because I wanted to find out why you left without saying good-bye."

"You didn't say good-bye to this pretty little thing?" Ed asked, with disbelief expressed through his voice. Caden just shrugged him off without even glancing at him.

"Last night you said that I saved you and helped you see that you had been lost in your past. I want to keep helping you."

"And what is it that you think I can do for you in return?" Caden asked

"Nothing, I just want to help you," I answered.

"If you can't think of anything that I can do for you, then you don't need me in your life," he concluded. Placing his hand on the door's handle, he opened the door to the outside world and said, "Find out what it is that you need in your life and pursue that treasure."

Paralyzed by his words, I asked, "What did you say?" I could feel my heart racing beneath my flesh.

"Good-bye, Gail," he said, and gently shoved me toward the door.

"Wait!" I ordered, and squirmed away from his overbearing hand. "I think that I need you in my life!"

"Why?"

"Because everything you say fits into my life's puzzle."

"Your what?" Caden asked in a frustrated manner.

"My grandfather used to say that everybody's life is a puzzle. We need to first find a proper foundation before we can add pieces to our lives. Once we have what we need, we can begin putting our picture together to make a story. Sometimes there are pieces that look like they will fit, so we try to force them, but something is just never quite right. We eventually have to keep trying new pieces until we find one that fits perfectly. Once we find the right one, our picture story to our life becomes clearer until we find our treasure in the end. And I think that you are a piece to my puzzle. A perfect piece that will help me find my treasure in the end."

"How does our story continue?" he asked curiously.

"I don't know. I guess it depends upon your decision," I said.

"If I fit into your puzzle, and I don't come with you, what would happen?"

"I know that answer," interrupted Ed. "The two of you will always have a missing piece in your life."

"Then who writes our story?" Caden asked Ed.

"You and God, of course," Ed replied.

"You can't have two writers to a story," I declared. "We decide what happens."

"Maybe we just need to open our eyes and see what is really out there," Caden said.

"Like the creator who decides the end result and the character who chooses the path to follow," Ed stated.

"What?" we asked in unison, as Ed's presence began to annoy the two of us.

"Just come with me," I begged and pleaded. "I can take you where you need to go. I'm not in a hurry to go where I was headed."

"How can I go with you when you can't even touch me

without hating what you feel beneath your fingertips?"

"Caden, it was a new feeling. I'm so sorry I hurt you, but I'm not disgusted by you. If I hated what I felt, why would I have chased after you?"

"I don't know," he replied.

"Close your eyes," I ordered.

"Why?"

"Close your eyes, man!" Ed shouted at him.

"Wow," I responded. "You better do what he says." I chuckled and smiled at Caden.

Slowly, he closed his eyes and waited patiently for me to respond. With my heart beating rapidly and my hands beginning to sweat, slowly and gingerly, I ran my hand through his thick dark hair until it reached the nape his neck. Slowly, I pulled him closer to my chest until I could feel it heaving against my own. Turning my head to the side of his cheek, compassionately, my lips touched his old wounds. With butterflies already alight in my stomach, I felt them stir as Caden firmly pressed the side of his face against my pursed lips.

"Um, I can take you back to the lodge if you want," grunted Ed.

"I'm sorry, Ed," Caden apologized.

"Oh, don't apologize. You can continue if you want," Ed stated with a grin.

"I just want to prove how much he means to me and that I am not turned off by the feel of him against my skin," I explained with embarrassment. I had forgotten completely about Ed in the seat next to us. "I was just trying to be affectionate with him so that he could see how attractive he really is."

"I think you proved that, babe," Ed commented. "I guess you're not coming with me then, Caden."

Taking a deep breath, with a smile imprinted upon his handsome face and a twinkle behind his affectionate eyes, Caden speculatively wondered aloud, "So where are we going?"

Chapter Twelve

"Turn here," Caden pointed out, gesturing toward a small gravel road smothered by overgrown weeds. The towering trees along the road guarded the entrance to the forest as if it were a secret hidden from the rest of the world.

"You said that nobody knows about this place except you?"

"At least I don't think anyone does. I've been coming here for years, and I have never seen anyone else here. It is like my own private paradise," he informed me.

"Paradise? It is a dirty gravel path with weeds. How much of a paradise can it be?" Gail wondered quietly. At times, Gail had a difficult time seeing past the surface of things. She had a tendency to take things the way they came, that is, until she met Caden. Other than her grandfather, Caden was the first person she ever desired to know from the inside.

The jeep rolled forward through the guarded entrance and into the darkened forest. One could only imagine what lurked within the shadows. I suddenly began to imagine myself in a spooky horror movie. I wasn't sure if I should fear Caden or hide behind him.

"Why is it so dark through here?" I asked him, but I was too afraid to look in his direction in case he happened to be cradling a hook in one hand.

"This is just the entrance. The trees block out the sunlight, but once we step through the forest, it is absolutely amazing. It is like somebody just carved it out of nature and placed it there just for me to find one day."

"Why do you say that?" I asked in an eerie tone.

"One day I was hiking along the road, and it was raining pretty consistently like this and..." He abruptly stopped in the middle of his sentence. "You have to park the jeep. We won't be able to take it any farther," he noted.

"Will it be okay here?"

"I told you, nobody knows about this place."

"Okay," I nervously agreed, and turned off the engine. "I'll just follow you."

"As I was saying earlier," he continued, as we huffed our way through the briars and weeds, "it was raining and I was cold. I kept praying that I would find a place to sleep and dry off. So I went off the main road slightly and stumbled upon the path. I followed it until it brought me here," he finished, just as we reached the end of the path. He pulled back the overhanging roots and vines that had wound their way around a large oak tree. They seemed to create a canopy above the entrance to our paradise on earth.

"Oh, wow!" I exclaimed with overwhelming joy. "I can't believe nobody else knows about this place!"

When the canopy concealing the natural wonder was

pulled back, I forced my eyes to blink several times in order to make sure that I was not dreaming. As we stepped through the entranceway leading into the secret forest, it seemed as if we had stepped over an imaginary line between night and day. At first, everything was too eerie for my mind to even reconcile with the gloom surrounding the area. With one small step and a little bit of faith in Caden, the gloom had transpired into our own "Garden of Eden," a forest where the blissful tranquility of life's harmonious meaning could be reborn.

"This is the most beautiful place that I have ever seen! I'm surprised that you haven't painted it so that more people can experience it."

"If I painted this place, I would have a difficult time recreating something so serene. The only way to understand its beauty is to experience it yourself. Anyway, if others found this place, it wouldn't be as meaningful to me anymore."

"It probably wouldn't remain beautiful, either. Humans have a way of destroying everything wonderful in this world."

"Satan has a way of destroying everything wonderful. Humans just have a tendency to listen to him," he corrected.

After a moment's hesitation in still silence, I finally replied, "You're probably right."

"Come on! You have to check this out! Even the rain can't spoil its beauty. It is always sunny here."

Following Caden through the forested garden, I noticed how the light from above us shined though the tops of the pines and brilliantly illuminated our skin. Standing before me, Caden's skin glowed boldly against the light. His body was cast in an angelic appearance.

The warmth that infiltrated Gail's body could not be

explained in words for her. It was almost as if she had been living life as a corpse before that very moment, and suddenly life had breathed back into her cold body. Life had begun to take form inside her. Even her senses had been revived. She could truly feel her heart beat for the first time. Her attuned ears listened vibrantly as if they were listening to the melody of the birds for the first time. And the scent of the majestic pine trees immediately captured the attention of her breathing nose. But her eyes, they could not believe themselves, though they were witness to it all.

"Look at that waterfall! This is absolutely amazing," I said, astounded by its majestic beauty.

The mighty falls tumbled over the rocky bed of the river and pooled into a swimming hole beneath it. Eventually, it transformed itself back into a deep, wide, and powerful river that led the way out of the sanctuary. Though we were standing above the falls, Caden pointed out there was a hidden entrance to the side of the falls that led directly behind it.

"There is even a natural ledge that formed into the rock, and you can sit upon it to watch the falls topple over the edge and plunge into the pool below."

"Really? Let's go," I replied ambitiously, and rushed to the side of the falls. "That is a long way down."

"Yes, it is," he agreed, and grabbed me from behind. He swung me over his shoulder and danced and twirled in circles until we fell upon the mossy, pine-needled earth bed of the secret forest.

"There is something I want you to see first," he excitedly proclaimed.

"Well, let's go."

"We will as soon as I stop seeing stars," he chortled.

"Okay," I said, laughing at him.

Just upstream from the falls was a small circular grassland area surrounded by blossoming trees. Their petals of pink and white swiftly floated in a soothing wind until they cushioned themselves upon the tall, wild grass. The sun shined through the rain droplets until the entire grassland was charmed by the presence of a rainbow.

"I don't know how, but every time it rains, there is a rainbow. It kind of reminds a person of how much beauty there can be in the world, no matter how much gloom surrounds their life."

"It sure does," I agreed, hand in hand with Caden. I felt his eyes studying my body. His hand kept squeezing mine tighter and tighter.

Finally, he asked, "So, do you want to go swimming?"

"Swimming? Isn't it a little cold for that?"

"No, the water isn't too bad. Come on!" he shouted over his shoulder, as he ran back toward the waterfall in the opposite direction.

Instinctively, I chased after him. I couldn't see him through the forested trees, but I could hear his every move. Each time I stepped around one tree to grab Caden, he disappeared behind another. I felt like a reborn child playing hide-and-go-seek. When I caught up with him, he was standing near the edge of the water. Without warning, he disappeared beneath the falls.

"Caden?" I called, but did not receive a response. "Caden? Where are you?" I shouted again, but still nothing in return. "Caden!" I panicked.

"What?" he shouted from behind me.

Yet, when I whirled around to face him, he was nowhere to be seen. Suddenly, I heard splashing in the water below. Peering over the edge of the rock formation, I saw him staring back up at me.

"How did you get down there?" I shouted to him. "I thought you couldn't swim?"

"It isn't deep. See, I can stand in it," he said, as his body rose out of the water.

"Huh, where are your clothes?" I asked, turning my eyes away.

"I took them off. They are under the falls. Come on in."

"I'm not swimming naked with you," I responded, with flattery wrapped inside embarrassment.

"Why not? I've already seen you naked. You have a beautiful body," he objected to my embarrassment.

With my cheeks blushing, I shouted in return, "Well, it will be cold!"

"It isn't bad. You are just a chicken."

"I am not!"

"Come on then," he urged. "Go under the falls. You will see how I got down here."

"I will then. I'll be right there," I told him, and ducked under the falls. "Oh, wow!" I exclaimed.

"Neat, isn't it?" I heard Caden say from below.

"You just slide down it?" I asked him, as I peered over the sloping rock bed beneath the falls. Gradually, over the years, the water from the falls had cascaded down into the small cavern and formed a natural waterslide. The water had smoothed the rock enough to create a gentle sloping ride of twists and turns. It appeared to me as a small cave with a hole bored into it. It was even wide enough for two or three people to slide at a time, and it poured directly out into the river below. One could sit at the top and look straight down to the bottom.

"Yes, come on. I will catch you," he said.

"I don't need you to catch me!" I shouted to him, while taking off my clothes. "Okay, watch out!" I screamed and pushed off the far wall of the slide. "Ah! It is cold!" I shouted, as I popped up below next to Caden.

"It isn't that bad!" he shouted, as he twirled me around in the water. "Want to go again?"

"Yeah! I'll race you to the top!"

Time passed without a care to Caden and Gail. Emotions between the two of them surpassed the level of affection. Their hearts were beginning to beat almost simultaneously. Their bodies seemed to flow in rhythm. There wasn't a care in the world between them. To each other, their souls were the only two in existence. They were even beginning to hear their stories being told.

"Did you hear that?" I asked Caden.

"Hear what? It is just the water talking," he said, as he waded through the water and huddled up against my quivering body. "You are trembling."

"I'm cold," I said, wrapping my arms snugly around his wet body.

"A friend of mine once told me that sometimes when we think we hear something but when we turn to look and can't find anything, it may just be our maker telling our story through our souls."

"And what is the maker saying?"

"He is uncovering all the secrets of our hearts. Telling everyone the little details that we tend to leave out during our version of life," he explained.

"Do you think that is who I heard?" I wondered. "Can you hear him now?" I asked Caden.

"Yes, he is telling me not to do what it is that I am about to do," he said, as he brushed his hand across my cheek.

"What are you going to do?"

"This!" he shouted, as he twirled me around in circles beneath the falls. Pressing my body firmly against the rock wall forming the falls, Caden's lips passionately met with mine. I felt his body pulsating with fervor against my palpitating skin.

"God! How I want you," I uttered to him.

"I won't do that. Not yet. We can't do that," he said, kissing me once again. "I'll never do that until the right moment. Just hold me. Just hold my body against yours until night falls upon us."

"I can do that," I said to him, as his body sank deeply into my arms.

"This place is like my own sacred garden where nothing could be wrong. I call it my 'Garden of Eden.'"

Night settled quickly in the "Garden of Eden," but the peace continually outpoured its serenity throughout the dwellers of the land. Snuggled in constant content inside the walls of their cozy little tent, their embrace sheltered their hearts from pain and softened their hard-set minds. Their colliding worlds were beginning to rebuild their shattered lives, and not one storm of any kind could tear down the foundation they had constructed together.

Face to face, his hand resting softly upon the back of my neck, Caden quietly asked, "Can I tell you something without you getting upset?"

"Of course."

"It is about when we first met," he slowly confessed, with a slight break in his voice. I could feel the palm of his hand growing clammy. "I was watching you in the cemetery. I saw you at your grandfather's funeral, and I waited for you to come back. I waited because I knew you would come back. You looked just like I did the day I lost my wife and daughter. I knew there wasn't any way you could stay away from him for too long."

"Why were you there the day of the funeral?" I asked,

sitting up straight. I felt taken aback by his confession. My intimate privacy had been invaded.

"I was visiting my wife and daughter," he reacted, with a silent plea for mercy. "I heard your eulogy and was drawn to you. I wanted to know more about you.

"Then, the next day I watched you from a distance. The way you approached the fawn when you were so hurt just showed me how deep of a person you were. I couldn't stop myself from helping you. Please don't hate me."

"Hate you? Why didn't you just talk to me?"

"I was afraid. I was afraid that if I talked to you, I would be forgetting my wife."

"This is creepy," I said under my breath and sat directly up in the tent. "It was you I saw in distance that evening, not the deer. Wasn't it?"

"Yes, it was me. Did I scare you away?" he asked, as I sat huddled in the corner of the tent.

"No," I responded with a bit of uncertainty. "I just can't believe I didn't pick up on it before now. When we spoke earlier, you said that despite my pain I still helped the fawn. Then, when we were trying to get it to the shelter, you told me to go get my jeep. I should have realized it then."

"The day we saved the deer, I wanted to help you with the shelter, but I just wasn't ready to go back to that life. The whole time I was standing there, I kept thinking that I was going to go home to my wife and child. In reality, though, I knew that it wasn't possible."

"So, you are afraid to live a different life."

"Yes, I don't want to go home to an empty house. I would walk through the door of my home and never hear the laughing voice of my daughter again. I don't think I could live without it."

"But you are living."

"It isn't the same," he said.

"I guess I know what you mean. I've always been living, but I never felt alive until I met you," I stated.

"Then you understand how in life you can experience death while still breathing."

"Yes, but we have to find something that makes you feel whole again," I told him. "What about when you saved that deer? Did you feel alive then?"

His face dropped, and his eyes rose to focus on mine. He firmly replied, "Without a doubt."

"Then why not continue feeling alive? Do what makes you happy."

"Because I'm afraid to leave them behind," he stated. "Aren't you afraid to let go of your grandfather?"

"Without a doubt," I declared. "Besides my brother, he was all I had left."

"What about your parents? What about the family you said you had in Clearwater?"

With tears forming in my eyes, I asked him, "Do you know why I saved that deer?"

"No," he stated with concern. His eyes overflowed with tears when he looked in my direction. Sliding himself closer to my body, he wrapped his arms around my shoulders and pulled me tightly to his chest. Cradling me within his arms, he rested his head upon mine and said, "You can tell me anything. I won't leave you. I won't run away. I promise. I never break a promise."

His words comforted me, and I believed he would never intentionally leave me. Though I was overwhelmed with emotion, it was the first time I had told anyone about the death of my parents. I don't believe I could have done it without him or the security of our garden. The warmth of life's light never stopped shining in "Eden."

"I saved her because I didn't want her baby growing up without a mother. I didn't want her to have to watch her mother die the way I did. People say that I was too young to remember the accident, but I can still see everything as if it were happening now," I began. The tears in my eyes stopped flowing as I began the journey to the past. It was a journey that I swore I would never take again.

"I can't remember too much before the accident or what happened directly after it, but I do know I watched both of them die. Sometimes I blame myself, but sometimes, like the others, I blamed my grandfather for playing God.

"I tried to convince myself that he didn't have a choice, but he did. He decided who lived and who died. I just wonder if my brother and I were meant to live."

"You're here, aren't you?" he pointed out.

"I'm here, but like you, I'm not really here. My whole life has been surrounded with death. I guess I died along with everyone. Before I met you, I don't think I ever felt my heart beat.

"When I stepped into this enchanted forest with you, I could breathe again. It is the first time that I have ever been able to tell anyone about the day that changed my life forever. Even if I wanted to talk to someone, they wouldn't listen."

"I'm listening. Tell me what happened to them."

"I was six, and my brother was about thirteen. My grandfather, Noah, was my father's dad. They loved the outdoors. There wasn't a thing they hadn't tried, from simple hiking and camping to rock-climbing. You name it, they probably tried it.

"When my mom met my dad, she became interested in the outdoors along with them. So naturally, when we came along, we followed in their footsteps. Every year, even when I was only a year old, we went on this extravagant camping trip. It began with us stopping at the lodge and staying overnight. Of course back then, according to Zachariah, it was only a camping ground. After that, we went canoeing and hiking along a river that led us to the same mountain that my grandfather had been climbing since he was a boy. He knew every old and new crack in that rock," I explained to Caden, who had been listening intently.

"And?" he questioned, when I stopped to observe his reaction to my story.

"So, we eventually made it to the mountain. One side was mostly solid rock, while the other side and the top were sloping hills covered with trees and smaller sections of rock.

"My grandfather was the lead climber, while my dad brought up the rear. Of course, I was too little to climb, so my grandmother, Mary, had come along to stay with me. Once they got started climbing, we hiked up the natural trail on the other side of the mountain and naturally beat them.

"Now, mind you, it was the spring, so as usual it had been raining quite often. Still, my dad and Noah decided that it would be okay to continue climbing.

"When my grandmother and I reached the top, she noticed that the very top of the hill was not very stable at all. She said it looked like it would collapse at any time, but there wasn't any way to warn them."

Interrupting with confusion, Caden asked, "So you were standing on the unstable hill, not a mountain?"

"Well, we weren't at the very top. There is an area where the trail ends just below the top, but you can't actually climb to the top. The area is a small ledge that gradually transforms from rock to soil and vegetation. It is hard to explain, but I can still see it clearly. It is probably the only reason I lived through the landslide."

"They died in a landslide?" he predicted.

"Well, by the time they were close enough to see how unstable the top was, it too late to turn back. My grandfather reached the ledge and climbed up next to my grandmother and me. Then, my brother climbed up. At this point, we heard a low rumbling."

"Get back under the ledge!" Gail's grandfather warned, but it was too late. As they were scrambling for shelter, the first of the slide occurred. Gail was directly struck by it and toppled over the edge of the cliff! On the way down, she caught hold of the lead guide rope with her right hand. She felt the rope burn off the flesh of her hand, so she let go in pain. As she felt herself falling, there was a sudden, sharp tug felt by her right hand once again. It was her grandfather! He had grabbed hold of her hand and yanked her to safety!

As he held her tightly in his arms, she could feel a frantic terror take hold and fill them. He kept looking from the ledge sheltering the others, and back to the mountain where her parents hung. He knew his wife was too frightened to move to help him. She just kept clutching Damien in her trembling arms. She wouldn't let him go.

Noah knew his grandson could help save them all, and Damien fought to break away from the hands that bound him to safety. But he was not strong enough. All he wanted to do was help his grandfather save his parents, but his grandmother, Mary, clung to him as if he were her lifeline.

"Don't you do it! Don't you leave them alone!" Gail heard her father yell from below. "Get her out of here. Get her to safety!" he called out. "Save my children!"

As Noah cuddled Gail close to his chest and turned to flee for safety, she glanced into her mother's eyes for the last time.

"She knew she was going to die. I could see it in her eyes."

"I'm so sorry. That was one thing I didn't have to witness. I never had to look into my family's eyes as they died," Caden said to me in sorrow.

"By the time we reached the safety of the ledge, the rest of the landslide hurled itself down upon us. We were buried alive, but my parents weren't so lucky. They were buried in death.

"It took till nightfall to dig us out. It took a week to find their bodies. Nobody knew where they landed, since they crashed to the earth with their killer and washed away with it," I told him.

What bothered Gail most was not reliving her parents' death, but the fact that she didn't shed a single tear when she spoke about the accident nearly twenty years later. She wondered if she had forgotten how much she loved them?

"Gail, I don't know what to say. I'm so sorry you had to witness that, especially at such a young age."

"You know, I think I am okay. I didn't think that I could ever tell anybody about this, but I feel more relieved than anything. I guess I was more afraid of what might happen if I told somebody about the past; is that wrong?"

"No, I don't think it is wrong," he confessed. "After the death of my family, I got so tired of explaining what happened to people that I just snapped. I didn't want anyone's pity or sympathy and began to hate my family and all my friends. I started to hate my wife and daughter for dying. So, when I left, I told myself that I would never tell anybody about their death again. I was so afraid that I would hate them again.

"Then, when I met you, I was more afraid that you would hate me. I thought you would think of me as some kind of monster."

Directing his face toward mine, I clearly stated, "I would

never think that, ever."

Whispering in my ear, he asked, "Can I hold you all night? I don't want to let you go."

"I don't want to let you go, either. I never want to lose you."

"Please, stay with me," he shyly choked. "I won't do anything you don't want me to."

"It's okay," I comforted.

"I just want to be closer to you. I just want to feel myself closer to you," he uttered quietly.

"It is okay," I nodded nervously. "I want to be closer to you, too."

Chapter Thirteen

"So where are we going?" I asked Caden the next morning when we had arrived back at the jeep. We found it waiting in the exact location we had left it. Not even a leaf or speck of dust left its trail behind. The atmosphere outside the sanctuary seemed calmer and more pacifying compared to the day before. Perhaps it was because we had found a place to escape from the rest of the overbearing world, and nobody possessed the power or knowledge to find us. "Eden" had become our own hidden hollow, and it would always remain in secrecy.

Leaving the sanctuary of our little garden burdened my already present torments. A part of me desired to hide away with Caden in "Eden" until the end of our time; yet, I knew the anguish of our problems would eventually find us. There isn't a soul in the world who can hide from the torture of reality's sin. No matter how far we run or how long we hide, it will find us. There is no escaping until we confess it is near.

"Are you sure you're not in a hurry?" he asked.

"No, why?" I questioned. I really wasn't in a hurry, but I did have some place to be.

Surprised, he asked, "You're not expected by your family?"

"No, they don't know I am coming."

"Oh," he acknowledged, his eyes revealing suspicion. One could always grasp his communicating thoughts by reading his facial expressions alone. "Well, if you are not in a hurry, would you like to come with me to White Salmon?"

Pleased by the invitation, I turned to him with a radiant smile and said, "I would love to come with you." I wasn't excited about my trip to Clearwater, anyway.

"Really?" he said with excitement.

"Yes, I could use some time away from everything that has been going on."

"Great, because I would love to show you the cabin where I stay."

Slightly rolling down the window of the jeep, for the first time in several days, I heard the sound of birds chirping outside our "garden of Eden." Even the sun could partially be viewed through the lingering clouds that insisted on hovering nearby. It lazily poked its head out from underneath its cozy white and fluffy blanket of cotton. Opening its eyes wider and wider, it stretched and stretched until it found a comfortable seat high above the mountain peaks. Shining brightly, it led the way through another day.

"Are you still tired?" I asked Caden, watching his head bob back and forth.

Rubbing his tired eyes he replied, "A little bit. It has been awhile since I have had a good night's sleep."

"Well, if you tell me the easiest way to go, I can probably get us there without any trouble. I could always wake you if I have a question."

"Are you sure?"

"Yes, I'm fine. Go ahead and relax. The seat even reclines," I grinned.

"Okay," he said, shaking his head. "Just stay on route ninety until it changes to route eighty-two and follow that all the way to route ninety-seven. I'll probably be awake by then and can guide you the rest of the way."

"Ninety to eighty-two to ninety-seven. Got it," I declared.

"Are you sure you are okay with this?" he asked one last time. "I mean, this is completely in the opposite direction that you were headed."

"Like I said, my family has no idea that I am even on my way to see them. I haven't even seen them since the day after my parents' funeral," I said, before I realized I let half of my secret slip out.

"Really, why?"

"It is a long story that will put you to sleep," I said, trying to cover my tracks.

"I think I would like to hear it. I'm ready for a nap anyway," he coaxed.

"I promise I will tell you later," I sighed. "Right now I need to concentrate on my driving."

"It is that bad, huh?"

With Caden snugly sleeping, the silence crept in and out until it had circled the jeep many times over. The dull, somber atmosphere was enough to drive a sane person mad. My attuned ears began to focus on anything that served as a reminder of living life.

The sound of the tires rolling on the impenetrable concrete began to function as a reminder of the passing day.

As the rotation of silence spun around us, my lips persuaded my mind into believing that I had symptoms of aphasia. I was a prisoner in my own body, a prisoner who lacked the ability to express my deepest regrets. In more direct words, the nostalgic decision I made to forget the reason I left my home in Opportunity seemed to be taunting my every nerve. Yet, as I followed the road ahead of me, I still could not see where the signs pointed.

I remember it being the brightest of all the signs on the highway. The shiny green sign even reflected the sun through the windshield as if it were trying to flash my attention. It stretched high toward the sky, looking down at the valley below that supported the slender trees rooted within its ground. The pretentious sign displayed its worth by towering over the rest of the valley as if it were the queen casting orders meant to be followed. It read "stay right toward Seattle, exit left to route eighty-two toward Yakima."

I turned left, though on the other side of Seattle was Clearwater. My mind second-guessed my decision, but my heart pressed forward. I was going to travel as far as I could with Caden by my side.

I was glad Caden lay sleeping next to me and unaware of my second-guessing thoughts. Every now and then, in between watching the road, I kept sneaking a peek at him sleeping next to me. His round cheeks jiggled with each bump in the road, and his smile widened the farther we traveled together. I couldn't help but wonder what he dreamt. I hoped he would tell me what made him so happy.

"Hey," Caden remarked, when he finally awoke a couple of hours later. "Where are we?"

"We are just getting ready to merge onto ninety-seven."

"Perfect timing," he said, referring to his timely wake-up.

"Yeah," I agreed without emotion. I kept thinking about

how I should have been traveling north instead of south. I was angry at myself for using Caden as an excuse for my delayed trip back home.

"Are you okay?" he asked with concern.

"I'm just tired," I informed him, but I meant I was tired of arguing with myself.

"We can pull over if..."

Interrupting, I apologized with remorse, "No, I'm sorry for interrupting you, but I should be okay for a little while. I'm not that tired."

"You're still wondering why you persuaded yourself to come with me. I can tell. Everybody has their reasons, and every reason is as good as another. You don't have to explain anything to me."

"I should, though. After everything you have shared with me, I should be willing to explain why I am dreading the trip back home. It is just difficult because of everything that has been happening lately. It is just one thing after another, and I keep using every little detour as an excuse not to think about the things that keep bothering me. I'm always looking for a way out."

"It is understandable. Don't worry about it. At least you can admit the problems to yourself," he replied light-heartedly. "Are you at least getting hungry? My stomach is the only thing I keep thinking about right now."

"Yeah, I could go for something to eat, but how much farther do we have?"

"Another hour or so," he answered. "We can stop if you want."

"I'm really just tired of driving. Do you want to drive?"

Shaking his head in trepidation, he stated, "I don't drive, not since the accident."

"Why?"

"Because I don't want to kill anyone," he coldly announced. His emotionless behavior perturbed me. His mixed emotions were very perplexing. One minute he was ready to become a new man, the next, he was back to believing he was a murderer.

"How long have you been rehearsing that line? You said it so calmly and collectively that if I didn't know better, I would have believed that you actually killed somebody."

"I've thought about it ever since that day. I just don't want to hold another life in my hands. I don't want that kind of power."

"You are being ridiculous. You know that accident wasn't your fault. There is nothing you could have done to prevent it. Even if you never took your eyes off the road, that deer would have been nearly impossible to spot. You have to stop blaming yourself for things that were out of your hands."

"You are one to talk about not blaming yourself and others," he deducted. "It is part of the reason you won't talk about your family, isn't it?"

"Yes it is," I said, glancing quickly at him. "It isn't that I don't want to tell you, but it is difficult for me understand why things happen the way they do. I'm the type of person who likes to figure things out on my own. When I find the answer, I will be ready to talk about it, especially with you."

"We are very much alike, you and me," he admitted. "I think that I could fall in love with you, but I don't know if this is the best time. I don't think it will work if neither of us can focus on one another," Caden stated.

"I don't know if there ever is a bad time to express love," I pointed out in return. I wanted him to love me.

"You don't think?" he asked. "Pull over then," he ordered.

"What?"

The Woodcarver's Hand

"Pull over," he repeated.

Pulling to the side of the road, my heart began to ache. I could barely breathe. My lungs heaved in agony. I didn't know what I had said to make him angry.

"Caden," I called to him, as he stepped out of the jeep through the passenger door. "Wait! What are you doing?" I cried, as the door closed behind him, but to my surprise he walked around the front of the jeep and opened the driver's side door.

"Move over," he commanded, as he slid next to me.

"Okay," I said with confusion, climbing into the other seat. "What are you doing?" I nervously asked, as he positioned himself on the seat and closed the door behind him.

"Shh, I have to concentrate," he said, putting his hands on the steering wheel.

"On how to drive?" I asked with concern. "You don't have to drive if you haven't in awhile, especially if your license isn't current. We don't want a detour to jail."

"You worry too much," he replied, and pushed my seat back into the reclining position.

"Ah!" I screamed. "What are you doing?" I laughed in question of his sanity.

"I have no intentions of driving. I like hitching much better. You never know what kind of beautiful lady you will pick up," he said, climbing through the front of the jeep and lying on top of me.

"Or what kind of psycho you will pick up!" I shouted, playfully punching and tickling his ribs.

"I'm not a psycho. I just want to spread my love."

"I thought this was a bad time to spread our love."

"It is never a bad time to share our love," he commented.

"So, shut up and kiss me already."

101

Chapter Fourteen

The sun was beginning to settle behind the sheltered cabin in the woods by the time we had arrived. The hand-built cabin sat tucked within the hills just outside a nearby mountain range, which ran along the Columbia River. Its surroundings included several woodcarvings of different animal species, including man. The larger carvings consisted of brilliant designs and colors that seemed to blend with nature's surroundings. Each of their bases rested upon their own tiny tree stump that appeared to be still rooted deep within the soil. They appeared to be growing out of the ground itself.

"Who did these?" I asked in amazement.

"I painted them, but my friend Malachi carved them."

"Is Malachi the friend who dyed your boxers pink?"

"Yes," he laughed, "but I prefer to call him a friend who probably saved my life."

The Woodcarver's Hand

Together we walked to the front of the cabin and climbed up its wooden porch stairs. We did not enter the cabin right away. Instead, we followed the porch around to the back of the cabin and stopped when its landing reached an open field surrounded by a small lake. Waving his hand toward the edge of the back porch, Caden motioned for me to have a seat next to him on the steps leading to the backyard.

In the distance, the artistic sun sank swiftly into the cool water of the lake. Colors of golden yellow and scarlet red laced the sky with their beauty. Slowly, they began to fade as the lake's thirst was quenched by the fire of the bright orange ball in the sky. Soon, all of the tranquil light surrounding us disappeared behind the black cloak of night.

"We should go inside. It is getting pretty chilly out," Caden said.

"Oh, sure. Are the sunsets here always this beautiful?"

"Not always," Caden replied, as he opened the back door, "but when they set over the lake like that, it is hard not to find them beautiful."

"It is kind of dark in here," I observed. The only visible light in the cabin seemed to be coming from the living room. "Is your friend not home?"

"Oh, he is home," Caden said, as he led the way through the cabin. "He is just always in the dark. Right, old man?" Caden said, as he tapped the back of the wooden chair his friend sat upon.

"It is good to see you again, my friend," the man said.

I could tell right away that there was something very different about him. In his left hand, he clung tightly to a wooden walking stick, which appeared to have animals carved about its base. He was old, very old, but not weak.

"It is good to see you, too," Caden said, as he gave the man a hug.

"You've shaved," Malachi said, as he felt the scars on Caden's face. "And you've brought home a friend, a lady friend," he concluded, without even touching me.

"How did you know I was a lady?" I asked him.

"I'm very old and blind. I know what a woman smells like, and it is much better than a man," he answered. "Now come and give me a hug. Any woman who can get this man to shave deserves a hug."

"I am Gail," I said, giving the man a hug.

"Your stomachs are growling," he said, as he rose out of his chair. "I have plenty of soup and apple pie leftover from my dinner. Come on in to the kitchen."

"So how have you been, Malachi?" Caden asked him, as we followed him into the kitchen. "You look like you have been busy over the past month."

"Oh, you know me. There is always something to keep me busy," he said, as he pulled the pot of soup from the refrigerator. "Like straightening up my house after you leave. You can't move a blind man's furniture."

"I'm not that bad," Caden remarked.

"You watch, sweetheart, by tomorrow evening I will be tripping and fumbling all over this cabin just to get to the bathroom."

"It isn't that easy to live with a blind man, either. You're always confusing my stuff with yours."

I couldn't help but laugh as I watched the two of them bicker back and forth. They reminded me of two brothers fighting over who was right and who was wrong. Malachi was a little interesting to observe. He could move back and forth as if he could see every part of the world before him.

"Like what?" Malachi inquired. "If you would put your stuff away, then I wouldn't grab it by mistake."

"Like my boxers," Caden replied.

"What?" Malachi asked.

"The white ones that are now pink," I reminded him. "He let me wear them."

"Oh, those," Malachi remembered. "They don't look any different to me," he teased. "And you are supposed to be on my side," he said to me. "I'm the poor defenseless blind man that every woman should look out for."

"Oh, I see," I joked. "What do I get in return for being on your side?"

"Food," Malachi answered, as he set a bowl of soup before me. "And no crack on the behind for wearing the boxers from a man you just met."

"Well, that is a good benefit," I agreed. "Don't move the man's furniture, Caden. He is a poor defenseless blind man."

"Hey," Caden whined.

"Well, you really shouldn't leave your stuff out. He could get hurt," I stated.

"Great," Caden said, "now I have to listen to both of you. You may be siding with Malachi about this, but you're still sleeping with me tonight."

"Nobody is sleeping with anybody in this house if they aren't married," Malachi stated. "Call me old-fashioned, but that is the way it is going to be."

"Well, I didn't actually mean she was going to sleep with me. I just meant in my room with me."

"She may be sleeping in your room, but not with you. You can sleep in the loft," Malachi stated. "Besides, I know she hasn't slept with you yet. She doesn't stink like you. She still smells as good and ripe as this apple pie," he said, as he held it up before us.

"Yeah, nice comment, Mr. Old Fashioned," Caden responded.

After dinner, the night quickly slipped away, and we

clumsily made our way to bed. Instead of choosing Caden's room to sleep in, I chose to sleep in the loft above the living room. Its only sleeping arrangement was a feather-stuffed mattress on the cold hardwood floor. At first, I thought it was foolish of me not to take Caden's room, but after awhile I didn't mind sleeping on the floor. In fact, the homemade mattress felt extremely comfortable. The only thing that kept me awake all night was the bright light of the moon beaming through the small skylight window above me. It was beautiful, especially with the fireplace crackling below. It reminded me very much of the camping adventures I used to have as a child. The only thing missing was my family. I felt alone and isolated from them by fear.

"Hey," came a surprising voice from the top of the loft stairs. Unable to sleep, Caden had sneaked out of his room and climbed in bed with me.

Gail was relieved by Caden's presence, and Caden felt safe in Gail's arms. Most of the night slipped away due to their constant conversing. They couldn't help but seek out every detail entrapped within each other's souls.

"I can't believe I just told you that," Caden said uneasily. "I'm so embarrassed."

"Oh okay, John Caden Evert."

"What? You don't believe me?" he asked, staring at the flickering fire flames dancing across the wooden beams lining the roof of the cabin.

"It isn't that I don't believe you," I began with an uncontrollable laugh, "I just have a hard time believing your father was a minister." I concluded with a snorting laugh, "Especially after what you just told me what you dreamed about in the car."

"Did you just snort?" he asked, laughing out loud. "And I told you that because I didn't think you would make fun of me."

"Shh," I warned. "You'll wake Dad, and he'll chase you back to bed," I teased. "And I won't make fun of you. Just hope Malachi doesn't find out about your little fantasy involving the two of us, or something that you are fairly well attached to might come up missing."

"Shut up! He isn't that bad," Caden laughed hysterically. "Just don't tell him we went skinny-dipping!"

"Will he spank you, too?"

"He might," he nodded, "but he is a good guy."

"How did you meet him?" I inquired. "You said he saved your life. How did he do that?"

"He did save my life. I wouldn't be here without him," he praised. "When I took off, I didn't have any place to stay other than the lodge. I stopped in and asked him for water one day, and he offered me a place for the night. We have been friends ever since. No," he corrected himself, "he is more than a friend. He is family. The only family I really have left."

"What about your father and mother?"

"My mom died when I was eighteen, and my father lost his faith after that. He took to drinking and never made anything of himself. I haven't seen him since I was about thirty. It has been nearly fifteen years. I wouldn't even know where to look to find him. He could be dead for all I know."

"That is awful! What did your mother die from?"

"She had breast cancer. Back then, they didn't catch it until it was too late. It spread to her bones, and she died. There was nothing anybody could do."

"I'm sorry," I empathized. "My grandfather died of esophageal cancer. Well, not really esophageal cancer. He didn't know he even had a problem until he couldn't swallow. He went to the doctor, and they thought he had Barrett's syndrome, but they found a tumor."

"What is Barrett's syndrome?"

"It is where the stomach acid backs up into the esophagus and basically eats away at it. The esophagus gets so tight that it is hard to swallow and needs to be stretched."

"So they found the tumor when they were stretching the esophagus?" he asked.

"Yes, so they decided to operate but stopped when they found out it had spread to his other organs. They did treatments, but they said it was so far advanced that he had only a five-percent chance of survival over the following year. But he hung on for five years."

"Why such a little chance?"

"It is just a type of cancer that spreads quickly; because it isn't associated with pain, nobody ever knows there is something wrong until it is too late."

"I'm sorry. I know what it is like to watch someone die."

When I was finally able to explain the death of my grandfather to Caden, my body was filled with a calming relief. A heavy burden had been lifted. Even after everything we had been through, it took that long to discover that talking to him about my life and the trials within it wasn't going to be as difficult as I initially thought. He could understand and relate to everything I had been through. It was amazing how our lives seemed to melt together.

"So Gail, what is your full name?" Caden finally asked, after a lapsed moment of silence.

"Gail Grace Rein. I don't think that it flows. The names don't sound like they belong together, but Grace was my mother's middle name, so I guess it fits."

"I think it sounds great together. It is a perfect fit. Gail sounds like the storm tossing upon the ocean, while God's graceful hand keeps a tight rein upon it. It is by God's grace

The Woodcarver's Hand

the storm is kept under control," he explained.

"I never thought about it like that before."

"You should," he advised, and rolled over onto his side in order to kiss me upon the cheek. "I think that I am in love with you. I can't explain the feelings I have for you in any other way," he admitted. Then, he softly asked, "Can you explain love to me?"

Thinking the question over for a moment, I offered an answer by explaining the intimate feelings I felt for him. "Love makes you realize there are more things in life to think about. It is this sensual feeling that you never want to lose, so you don't want to do anything to change how it feels."

"Yes," he agreed. "When I look at you, I remember how great it feels to be alive and have something to look forward to. I don't want to lose that feeling. When I look at you, I want to see your smile and remember how good it feels to want you."

"To want and feel something other than the urge to see your wife and daughter one last time?" I asked him.

"Yes," he whimpered, "every time I look at the world, I realize that I'll never see them in it again."

In tears I added, "And no matter how hard you try, you can't ever remember exactly how their smile looked or how wonderful it felt to hold them in your arms. You just wish that you had paid more attention to those little things when they were alive, because you'll never have the chance again."

"Every time I look at playground filled with laughing children, I wish that I would have taken her to one more often when she was alive. I hate the fact that I was always too involved with my work."

"When I'm at the shelter or the recreation center, all I can think about is the death of my parents and my grandfather. I want to change everything about the buildings and all the routines that go on there so that I don't have to be reminded of them."

"But at the same time, you don't want to forget about them. You don't want to change anything. It gets to the point that you don't even want to get out of bed in the morning. All you want to do is dream of them so that you don't ever have to wake to reality."

"I miss them so much!" I sobbed.

"Please, don't leave me alone like they did," Caden cried in my arms. "I don't think that I could handle losing you."

"I'll never leave you," I cried in return, but at the same time I thought it was an impossible promise to keep. I just didn't want him to hurt anymore.

Diary: A new day

5 June 03

Mark 4:9 "He who has ears to hear, let them hear..."

Tomorrow —a word for today gone wrong. No matter how our day proceeded, we as humans believe that tomorrow is the cure for the dying today and the already passed yesterday.

What if there weren't a tomorrow, and today was all we had left? If we knew today would be our last, what would we change about ourselves? What would you change— anything? What would you do? Would you say, 'I love you' one extra time? Would you kiss the one you love until you breathed your last breath? Would you prepare for your death? Or would you lie down and die, giving death its glory?

Perhaps the things we cherish most should not be forgotten but remembered daily.

Chapter Fifteen

Plop-plop-plunk! sounded the stones I tossed into the lake before me. I sat quietly still in the morning sun with my feet dangling off the boating dock. The reflection peering back at me through the water seemed empty. With each drop of a stone, the figure became more distorted. It seemed to cave and fold with each new stirring ripple.

"Reflections tell no lies," sounded Malachi's voice, as he thudded his way across the dock. It was as if he could see everything without actually seeing anything. It must have been his mind's eye speaking in turn.

"Morning," I said to him. "Have you seen Caden this morning? He was gone when I got up."

"Yes, he got up very early this morning to go see an old friend. I'm surprised that you didn't notice him leaving. After all, he did climb out of your bed this morning."

"Yeah, sorry about that," I said, blushing. "When do you

think he will be back?" I asked with jealousy.

"Soon," was all Malachi said, as he began to whittle away at a piece of wood within his hand. "He needs you, you know?" he sounded. "I heard the two of you talking last night."

"Yes, and I need him. I feel like he is meant to be a part of me," I cautiously added. I wasn't frightened of Malachi, but at the same time he made me nervous. It was as though he could see inside my soul. He reminded me a lot of my grandfather.

"Did you know that when two souls can hear their stories being told as one, they are meant to be together?" he inquired.

"No," I remarked. "I don't know about that."

"It is true. Of course, they only can truly be one when they allow their lives to become one."

"But how do you know for sure that you are making the right choice with your life?" I asked him, hoping for more of an answer than my grandfather had left with me.

"Mmm," he sounded. "Have you ever seen a block of carving wood take form?"

"My grandfather used to carve all the time. He was very good at it and very proud of his work, perhaps a little too proud sometimes."

"Most creators are, but then sometimes they probably have the right to be. After all, they did work so hard to complete a masterpiece."

"I guess so."

"Then again, there is only one who has the right to brag about his creations and his talents. If it weren't for him, none of us would be here."

"You sound like my grandfather."

"I'm sure there is a good reason for it, too," he concluded. "Anyway, the hand of this woodcarver is very talented. I might add that his son was a wonderful carpenter himself."

"Really," I commented with disinterest.

"Yes, now pay attention," he scolded, and turned my head in his direction. "So, this creator sits down one day and writes a story. Within this story, he builds a character's identity. This identity grows as the story's plot thickens, as well as when the character in the story meets other identities from the past and present. Then one day the story is complete. Now all he has to do is make the character. So, he sits down and thinks about the story. He wonders what kind of person it would take to complete this story and what they should look like. Eventually, he figures out the perfect person to attach this identity to, so he carves them out. He has never been so proud, but something is wrong. He knows that this person won't be happy if he makes them do something that they don't want to do in their life. He doesn't want to be the bad parent scolding his children for not listening to him. He wants them to discover the truth about themselves on their own, so he gives them something called free will.

"Now comes the difficult part. What does the creator do with the story he just wrote? The character certainly won't follow it to the end. So, he creates paths. No chosen path is the wrong path, but only one is truly correct. He designs them so that one path leads to their true self. While the rest may seem right, in reality they just keep circling, and the character isn't getting anywhere. In order to move on, the character must first learn why he was brought to the situation he is in first.

"In the end, life is a puzzle waiting to be completed. Without completing the proper foundation, we can't build the rest of the picture in order to see and understand a part of our life. We must learn to understand the past and the present if we ever want to move onto the next chapter in order to solve the next puzzle of our life. If we ever want to see the true ending to our story, Gail, we must first understand what it is about."

With confusion I asked, "How do we know what it is about?"

"Oh, every story is different, and each puzzle in the story can only be solved by the main character within it," he remarked, still whittling away at the wood in his palm.

"Well, why do some stories have to be more in depth than others?"

"Everyone's story seems in depth to them. Only God knows why he makes other stories more involved than another. Some might say that it is just their personality, but I think that even God just gets plain bored sometimes and needs a little drama in his life," he said jokingly, with a deep chuckle. I couldn't help but laugh as I watched his little round cheeks wiggle with each roaring chuckle.

"Are you sure you never met my grandfather?" I double-checked. "You guys sound so much alike. I really miss him."

"I'm positive that I never knew your grandfather, and I can't take his place," he replied. "Though, I wouldn't mind getting to know you like a granddaughter."

"I would like that," I told him, "very much."

"Good," he said with a smile. "I just want to let you know that even though I never met your grandfather, I know he was a brilliant man."

"Why do you say that?"

"Because his character sounds an awful lot like mine," he acknowledged, holding a block of carving wood up to my face. "Would you like to learn how to carve?"

Chapter Sixteen

"Having fun?" Caden asked, when he had finally returned from his backwoods adventure. His entire outfit was covered in mud. Even his hair had managed to become entangled with the muck.

After watching him sit down and pry off his boots, I finally declared, "Apparently not as much as you."

"Yeah, I kind of fell down an embankment and landed on the bank of the river."

"Are you sure that is all you fell in?" Malachi questioned, with his nose turned up. "You stink."

"Gee, thanks a lot," the enthused Caden commented.

"I don't smell anything," I said, trying to make him feel better, although I had smelled better things in my life.

"Honey, when you are blind, your other senses tend to take over. Trust me, he stinks," Malachi assured me.

"Well, on a happier note, I see that you guys are getting

along well," Caden noted, as he turned the wooden figure in my hand around so that he could see it better.

"Yeah, he is trying to teach me to carve. My grandfather tried to teach me once, but I wasn't very good at it then."

"She still isn't," Malachi said.

"You can't even see it," I remarked, but he was right. In an attempt to carve a hand, which resembled my grandfather's carving hand, I had ended up with a lumpy oval shape with stick-figured fingers growing out from all angles.

"But I can feel it," he reminded me, as he made a quick attempt to steal the carving out of my hands.

"Oh, whatever," I said, and let the carving slip out of my hand and fall into the water of the lake. "So, what were you doing out in the woods, Caden?"

"Well, actually, I was visiting on old friend."

"What kind of friend lives out in the middle of the forest?"

"A friend that taught me how to fly," he stated with joy.

"I am going to go out on a limb and assume that you mean some sort of bird," I said to him. "Was it a bird that you had rescued?"

"She was an eagle with a broken wing. You can't be a figure of freedom with a broken wing, so I fixed her up and sent her on her way."

"What happened to her?" I wondered.

"She had been shot. When I examined her wing, I found two BB pellets in it. Probably a bunch of kids messing around who chose to do something foolish. I bet it was even on a dare," he explained.

"How long did it take her to heal?"

"It wasn't the healing she had a difficult time with, it was finding the courage to fly once again."

"And you helped her do it," I stated. "You can't get away

from them, can you?"

"I'm sorry?" he asked.

Interrupting, Malachi remarked, "I think that I am going to head inside and give the two of you a moment. I'll be inside if you need me," he mentioned, as he gathered his possessions and quickly, moving as fast as he could, scrambled out of the way. He seemed to be overreacting to the situation.

"Everywhere you go, there seems to be some sort of animal in need of your assistance. You even carry medical supplies around with you in your satchel. Don't you ever have second thoughts about helping them?" I asked Caden, who had hardly been plotting an excuse for his actions.

"No, I never have second thoughts. It is God and the animals who happen to have second thoughts about me," he cleverly disclosed. "I don't exactly go out of my way looking for animals to rescue."

"When you help them, how does it make you feel?"

"How do you think it feels?" he unkindly mocked. Then with a shrug of his shoulders, he said, "When you rescue an animal that you don't think is going to make it, your heart is left with an empty pit inside. But somehow you nurse it back to health and watch it take flight. All at once, you feel that pit mend and repair itself until you are whole again. It is one of the most amazing feelings that man can ever experience. You almost feel Godlike, but at the same time, you know that it was God's hand that helped you mend the bird's wing. It is then that you discover your place in this world. You know that you were designed for something special in this world."

Hearing his words caused my heart to ache in envy, not for Caden, but for the bird. Somehow, after everything that one man had done to her, she found the courage to place her faith back in another. In return, she found the freedom she needed in order to take flight once again.

"What made her fly?" I finally asked Caden, who was gazing intently up at the sapphire sky above us.

"It is amazing that the world is all under one sky, and we all look at the same sun but can still be in separate worlds," he said. "What made her fly, I don't know. I do know she is the lucky one, though. Her eyes will always see the world in a different perspective. While we look up, she looks down. She looks down into the heart of man. Perhaps that is why she fears us."

"Not all of us. She doesn't fear you. It was your hands that helped her live once again. She'll never forget that," I said. "And I don't think you will either."

"And you? Will you forget this moment? Will you forget about me?"

"I could never forget you. You help me see the world from a different perspective. Every day that I am near you, I feel my wings growing stronger, while the wounds grow weaker."

Taking hold of my scarred hand, he brushed the wound gently with the tip of his thumb and said, "It won't heal until you let go and fly in search of your freedom."

"And what about yours? Will it ever heal for you?"

"Not until I can I stare it in the face each morning," he said.

"I think that he is beautiful," I said, caressing his cheek. "And I would love for him to show the miracle within his touch."

"I would love to show you. I want to show you how she can fly in freedom."

Chapter Seventeen

"What's this?"

"It is a gift for you."

"What is it?"

"Just open it already," his voice urged.

Slowly but eagerly, my hands pried open the white cardboard box resting patiently upon my jittery lap. Just beneath the flap lay several crinkled pieces of yellowed newspaper. Cautiously tearing off the paper protecting the gift given generously to me, I revealed the wooden work of art in all its glory. It was the most amazing carving I had ever seen.

"Oh, wow! Malachi, did you make this yourself? It is absolutely amazing. I have never seen anything like it in my life. You have such a wonderful talent."

"Thank you," he said with a blush. "I kept trying to figure out what fit you perfectly, and that is what came to mind. So I carved it, and Caden painted it. I hoped you would like it."

"Oh, I do. It is beautiful!"

The small lifelike carving held within my hands represented a piece of my life's journey, which I could not express in words. Within my palms, I cradled a set of nurturing hands half the size of my own. Their natural look and tender touch created a sense of innocence in the world they surrounded. Yet, the most breathtaking feature of the rendition was the eagle. The brown and white bird of prey soared high above the hands, searching for his freedom.

"Sometimes it amazes me that someone who knows so little about a person can understand so much more," I commented, as I expressed my gratitude toward Malachi for helping me to begin to understand my story within this lifetime.

"It is hard for man to understand what it is that he cannot see," Malachi stated. "But for a man who has never had eyes to see out of, life becomes a world of passionate emotions to be expressed from the inside of his heart."

"And the eagle, what does it mean to you?"

"The way this bird of prey lives his life is the perfect example of how man should treat his freedom. He soars high above us all, while watching the world from afar. He is just waiting for his perfect opportunity to search for what he needs to survive. When what his heart desires is finally brought to him, he accepts it with gratitude. He does not care how big or little, how bad or good, or even how difficult or simple the situation may be. His heart does not dwell upon his choices. When the right time comes, he takes flight to a new freedom."

"I understand," I said from my heart. "She knows when it is time to be who she really is meant to be."

"Sure she does. She always has. All she needed was a little encouragement to fly."

"And she found it," I assured him with a hug. "So where is Caden? I'd like to see him before I go. I don't want to leave without saying good-bye."

"I'm not sure where he is. But you aren't leaving forever. I don't want you to forget about us."

"I won't forget about you," I acknowledged. "I just hope Caden isn't angry with me for deciding to do this on my own, especially after I pushed him into going with me."

"Nobody pushes anybody into anything. In the end, it is always the character's decision. He went with you on his own behalf."

"Well, I can't leave without saying..." I began, as the screen door upon the cabin swung open and slammed shut. The slamming was followed by the thudding of an angered man, whose feet pounded down the porch steps.

"Hey, what are you doing?" I asked him, as he threw a bag into the backseat of my jeep.

"I can't let you go alone," he informed me.

"What? Caden I have to do this alone, because when the accident happened, you were not a part of my life. I have to go back and fix things."

"You can't just go back in time and fix things!" he scolded. "I know because I tried. You have to start from where you are now. The past is the past and should remain in the past!"

"What is your point?" I snapped.

"Oh, boy," Malachi vocalized, and briskly walked away from the area. He quietly sat at a safe distance in order to watch the fight.

"My point?" Caden uttered. "My point is that I am a part of your life now, and we promised each other that we would never leave each other," he reasoned.

"Leave each other? I'm not leaving you. I'm coming back."

"How do you know that? How do you know that you won't get in that car, and I'll never see you again?"

"Because I told you I would come back to you."

"But what if you can't control it? What if you don't come back because you are taken away from me?" he quietly asked. His sorrowful expression of pain and guilt was overwhelmed with emotion.

"Then there isn't anything either of us can do about that. We can't change the outcome of situations that we are not in control of. We might have a choice about leaving or staying, but if it is our time to go, we are going to go no matter what decision we choose to make," I explained.

My own perplexing words baffled me. It was amazing how fast the truth came at me when I wasn't actually searching for it.

"Maybe there really is a certain order in which things must occur. Without an order, there would be nothing but chaos, and nobody would ever learn anything about this life," I examined aloud. Though many others had explained this over and over to me several times before that point, I guess I wasn't willing to accept and understand life until that day. Deep inside, I kept hoping there was more to life. I wanted life to be more than a written story meant to be acted out between characters. When this reality first hit me, it felt as though I were fictional. I had waited my whole life to discover that I was just a block of wood carved out to obey the orders of my maker... I felt like I was a slave.

"If our lives are already planned out, then why do we make promises if we really can't keep them," wondered Caden aloud.

"Maybe because we just choose to. Maybe it is a way that we show how much we care for each other. It is a way to remind others of how much love we possessed for them when we were there with them. We like others to know that we will do anything we can for them."

"Which is why I want to be there for you when you take the first step into the next chapter of your life," he explained. "Remember when we talked about the narrator of our lives?" he asked.

"Yes, I remember."

"Well, sometimes I sit back to listen and see if I can hear him. I used to hear my life just slipping away. The story was so sad when I reflected upon it. Now, just last night, I tried to hear what was being said about my character and his travels, but I heard nothing. What do you think that means?"

I understood what he meant, because I tried listening to that little voice inside my soul also. It was the night before I had decided it was time to move on, and I sat just outside the cabin, trying to persuade myself into thinking that I was making the right choice. Yet, no matter how hard I tried to convince myself that leaving Caden behind was the right decision, I couldn't hear any words of agreement from the little narrator inside of me.

"I never used to listen to my life's story, because it was never happy, either," I remarked. "I hated all of the events that had occurred within it. But when I met you, I thought that I heard a voice inside of me. It was as if the voice was writing about my life. I could hear him talking about the feelings that I felt at that moment and explaining every detail of that scene. He was speaking of all the hidden details in my heart. He wanted to express the things that I wanted to hide from myself and the rest of the world.

"But the other night, I sat on the porch and couldn't hear

anything, either. I just watched my life pass by that night; that is, until you showed up, asking me if you could join me. It was then I could hear my life being written once again. I think he was writing you into my life. I felt our stories becoming one," I declared.

"And I felt the same way," explained Caden. "I think God was just waiting for us to figure that part out on our own. You can't leave me now. Our stories will never be finished apart. You fit into my life's puzzle."

Chapter Eighteen

Looking through the rearview mirror, I watched the dust cloud over the long and winding drive. My eyes could barely penetrate the thick blanket smothering the recently traveled road behind us. The cloud of dusty smoke surrounding our turning tires dispersed into the atmosphere, where it surrendered to the sweeping wind. Only the eye within my passive mind could fathom where it might land.

From inside the truck, the distance revealed a multi-level white home placed next to a brilliant, scarlet-colored barn. Just before it galloped a young foal. Her sleek coat painted streaks of white across the red of the barn. Her young spirit raced the circling clouds moving throughout the valley, which spread wide before the majestic mountains placed high in the sky.

Her angelic ambition churned the past memories of my childhood dreams, which had become lost within the once hidden vault entrapped within my yearning heart. During that moment, I could still remember as a child, racing the wind to the imaginary finish line tucked within the shadows of grasslands. During the race, I became completely empowered by a young mare horse determined to beat me as well as the seeping wind. As she brushed past my shoulder and galloped into the cool breeze, I marveled at her tenacious ability to pursue the impossible.

Even now, I can clearly see the mare crossing the finish line with the wind licking her shoes, and the grass blades of green and gold reaching out to congratulate her on her victory. She had done it. Though the idea of beating the wind in a race to the finishing end seemed inconceivably hopeless, her heart's desire carried her across that imaginary line of triumphant achievement.

"It is strange to come back to the place that changed my life forever," I mentioned aloud to Caden, while still looking back toward the field through the rearview mirror of the jeep. "It is difficult because I promised myself that I would never back down to any challenge I came across in my life, but it is obvious that it was one promise I could not keep."

"You are here, aren't you?" he reminded me, without expecting an answer. He was simply trying to help me recognize the fact that I had found the courage to begin facing my fear of returning home. In actuality, I was not backing down on that promise I had made to myself many years earlier.

With the truck door ajar, my ears listened to the clanging clatter of dishes rattling inside the kitchen of the house. A familiar sound of a woman's voice echoed throughout the farm; yet, it sounded deeper and older than what I had remembered as a child. Even though their age had grown, nothing else about their life seemed to have changed with it.

The Woodcarver's Hand

Twelve o' clock and lunch had begun on time. Afternoon chores are soon to follow, I thought to myself, as I slammed the truck door behind my back, leaving Caden behind to wait patiently for my return.

Neither Caden nor Gail could imagine the outcome of their voyage that day. Together, both of theirs hearts seemed to race rapidly throughout their bodies, as if trying to keep the life circulating inside of them. With each foot Gail placed upon the rickety floorboards of the old porch, theirs hearts struck harder and harder in order to make sure their bodies were fully aware.

It was only moments later when an older woman with pepper-colored hair stepped onto the front porch. She meticulously dried her hands with the dish towel strategically placed upon her left shoulder and stood in silence while observantly staring at me in disbelief.

"Where have you been?" she finally snarled. "Get over here right now! How could you just take off without letting anyone know?" she scolded, as she smacked me on the shoulder with her wet dish towel.

"Ouch!" I cried.

"Damien finally called us two weeks ago to tell us that you were on your way up to see us. It doesn't take two weeks to drive across the state of Washington. Now where have you been?" she firmly demanded to know, as she continued to thwack me with her dish towel. "You should have called somebody to let them know you were okay! Tell me what you have been doing."

"Ouch! Give me a chance to explain," I desperately pleaded with her.

"Joan!" my grandfather, Tom, shouted, as he stepped out onto the front porch. "Give the child a break. It's something we haven't done in years," he mentioned as a side note.

"Now, go on and explain yourself," he urged, while peering into the jeep and shooting Caden a wary glare out from the corner of his eye. He never was keen on strangers. I knew he would be in a very contentious mood when he found out about Caden, but I thought it was time for them to understand that I was not a child anymore. They had chosen to miss that part of my life.

"Well, for starters, I didn't think I was on a time limit. I needed to just get away for a while and think," I began. "Then I met Caden, and we just connected. I decided to go home with him for awhile. That's all."

"That's all," Tom repeated. "Now I'm going to smack some sense into you. What is the matter with you? You don't go sleeping around with men that you don't even know. You especially don't leave your family in the dark when we are worried sick about you!" he shouted.

"Leave you hanging in the dark?" I calmly and quietly repeated directly in his face. "First of all, we haven't slept together, and if we decided to have sex, it would be between the two of us only. Second of all, you haven't been a part of my life for nearly twenty years. I didn't really think that anybody even cared about what I did," I rudely commented, without thought or care for their feelings. My emotions were surging. I felt as though they were judging me the same way they had judged my grandfather when he was alive.

"Gail, I am shocked that you would even think that we didn't care what happened to you!" my grandmother, Joan, remarked in an astonished manner. She was completely oblivious to the feelings of abandonment Damien and I felt. "Of course we care and worry about you. We have always wanted to be a part of your life. It is Noah we don't particularly care for. He stole you from us, and you and your brother chose to stay with him all these years. We thought you hated us for not being there for you that dreadful and unmentionable day long ago."

My jaw dropped. I was at a loss for words. I tried to force myself to speak, but I couldn't force out any words. The only sound emitted from my body was the breathing of my wheezing lungs. Their ignorant statement finally revealed the truth in their lack of knowledge toward my visit.

Behind me, I heard the jeep's door open and close. Finally stepping forward, Caden suggested, "Maybe we should go inside and sit down. I think everyone is just a little tired and a little confused about the entire situation."

"Mister, you have no business..." Tom began, but was immediately cut off as I came to my senses.

"Yes, he does. He is a part of my life now. If you are going to be also, you need to accept the changes that have occurred within it. I'm not six years old anymore. And I really agree with Caden that we should go inside and sit down, because what I am about to tell you is probably going to shock you," I finally revealed. With Caden by my side, I felt unstoppable. I finally felt in control of my life.

"Oh, dear Lord! She is pregnant!" Joan uttered in disbelief.

Well, for a moment, she felt in control of her life.

Stumbling forward into the kitchen, the faded colors of history emerged into the light and painted flashy memories upon the withering walls of papered flowers. These childhood memories obscured time's presence in my life for countless moments wrapped in precious seconds. Their existence became unaltered by time's condition and floated though my life's atmosphere unharmed by reality. As if it were only yesterday, I watched my young feet tap dance through lilies of the grasslands rooted deep within the walls of our sheltering home. I can remember just lying upon my back, pretending I was twisting and twirling through an imaginary field of never-ending flowers—a field where every childhood dream always came true in the end.

And now, I stand among a field of wilting dreams surrounded by a decaying life. If only my wandering feet had not become lost upon their journey...

"What is it that is so important that you had to come all the way up here to tell us? You could have called us," Tom suggested without thought or concern. I was beginning to suspect that I had approached the entire situation in the wrong manner. I came to make amends with my family, and I ended up starting an entirely new dispute.

"You aren't pregnant, are you? I mean, he is cute, but you hardly know each other," Joan remarked, once she calmed her emotions.

"No!" I snapped. "I'm not pregnant. We aren't having sex! And so what if we were. Who cares? He is forty-five, and I am twenty-five. We can make our own decisions."

"Did you hear that?" Joan said, as she turned toward Tom. "They are twenty years apart."

"Ahh!" I groaned. Feeling frazzled, in a harsh tone I asked, "When Damien called you the other day, that was the first time that you had heard from him, right?"

"Well, yes. We were so relieved to hear from him. We thought that the two of you had finally come to your senses and decided to come home to us, but then he told us that you had left because you were going through a difficult time back home," Tom answered.

"He said that you were on your way up here so that you could just get away for a while," Joan added.

"No. Well, in a way that is true. Damien was supposed to call you three weeks ago, not two. It explains why you didn't come to the funeral. I thought you were so selfish and hung up on the fact that you had won the battle that you just didn't bother to come."

"Honey, what funeral are you talking about?" they asked in unison.

"Noah died about three weeks ago," I disclosed. "That is why I needed to get away and come find out why you didn't come to the funeral."

"Well, we would have come. We didn't know," Joan replied.

"Because that jerk Damien never called you, and here I hated the two of you the whole time."

"You hate us?" they cried, but I wasn't concentrating on them. I kept thinking about how upset Damien had pretended to be the day of the funeral when Tom and Joan didn't show up. He lied to me.

Gail felt betrayed, and Caden could sense her emotions, but he wasn't going to let her lose control after how far she had made it.

When I didn't answer Tom and Joan, Caden clarified the statement for me. "She doesn't hate you. She was just looking for answers."

"Gail?" Tom called for my attention. "Well, how did he die?"

After mute moments of hushed silence, I finally offered an answer. "It was cancer. He had treatments, but there was nothing anybody could do."

Nobody spoke. Their motionless bodies sat in perfect content. They appeared to be unmoved by my statement, so I continued with truthful drama. I had hoped I would receive some sort of reaction from them.

"We knew he was going to die, and we kept preparing for it, but when we awoke the morning of his death and found him lying there...he was cold...and so stiff. It was something we weren't prepared to face.

"The night before, I wanted to tell him how the camp and shelter were doing and how grateful I was for having him as a grandfather...I wanted to tell him how much I loved him, but he just looked so tired. I just kissed him goodnight and told him that I would see him in the morning, but I didn't. I never got to tell him those things. It was too late the next morning. He died during the night, and nobody knew. He died alone.

"The damn disease ate him from the inside out. He was so miserable and alone," I explained to them, with only a single tear of emotion. I had been reliving the scene over and over in my head for so long that it just flowed out without much remorse.

"I am so sorry," Joan said. "How are we going to tell Mary about this?" she asked Tom.

"Grandma?" I whispered silently, so that only Caden heard my voice. "How is she?" I eventually asked out loud.

"Oh, honey, I don't know how to tell you this, but..."

"But what? What are you not telling me?"

Chapter Nineteen

"How long has she been like this?" I asked Joan, as we stood facing the back of my grandmother, Mary. She sat so still in her rocking chair that one would not even know she was alive. She looked as if she could have been a Victorian doll. A doll that just sat staring out her window, wishing to be alive.

"About a year now. Her mind just gradually started to go, and now she just sits and stares out toward the mountains," Joan explained.

"She doesn't remember anything?" I regretfully asked.

"No, not anymore. She rarely ever speaks to us anymore," she responded. "You know, I can't help but feel that some of this is my fault. We should have just let her go."

"What are you talking about? It isn't your fault. She just grew older."

"No, that is not what I mean. All she wanted to do was

hold you once again, but you never came. Neither you nor Damien ever came back to her. Every day...every day she wished that she hadn't said the words she did to you and your brother."

As Joan spoke of the regretful words spoken in hate from Mary one day long ago, I just couldn't remove my eyes from the dying woman in the corner of the room. How I felt the ache in her heart. How the desires of our heart can destroy us from the inside out.

As if on cue, the light from the window suddenly dimmed. I can still vividly see how the only light in the entire room seemed to be radiating off of her fading flesh. Though she looked so sad, her delicate skin seemed to glow so peacefully in the light of the day.

The irony presented to us that day was quite simple to see. Even as Mary sat dying in her private corner of the darkened room, she appeared to be the only one emerging alive in the light. The rest of us, Joan and I, seemed to be fading in the shadows of life's last pardon.

Bravely, I stepped into the light before my grandmother and turned to Joan to say, "I need a moment alone with Mary, please."

"Oh, certainly. Take as long as you would like, but do not hope for the best."

Do not hope for the best? What wonderful words of encouragement you have learned over the years, Joan.

Slightly tiptoeing across the room, I pulled the footstool of the rocking chair closer and slid it next to my grandmother. Her gaze held firm to the mountains outside her window and across the valley. For several minutes, I sat quietly next to her, admiring the majestic view. I understood why she loved it so deeply. It was one of the only pieces of her life that she could still see and hold close to her mind if she really desired.

"Grandma," I called, cupping her hand within my own, "it is Gail. Do you remember me?"

"Oh, hello," she greeted me with glee. It was the kind of joy a person expresses when holding someone they love for the very first time. It was pure happiness from a childlike heart. "Who are you, dear?" she simply and shyly asked, but without fear.

"Grandma, it is me. It is Gail."

"Oh, I don't think we have met before now. It is very nice to meet you. Is there anything that I can do for you?"

"No," I responded. "We have met before now. I am your grandchild."

"That is so nice to know. I didn't know that I even had a grandchild. Since I do though, do you think that you could help?"

"Yes, Grandma. I can help you," I told her with a smile, but it was only a false front. I kept wishing that I had come back to her sooner. Why did I wait so long to come and see you?

"That is so wonderful to hear!" she exclaimed with enthusiasm. Her hand clutched mine tightly and shook readily. "Nobody else seems to want to help me. They keep telling me that it is nothing important."

"What is it?"

"You see, I lost something out there," she said, pointing out the window.

"Out where, Grandma?" I didn't see anything but trees, the horizon, and the mountain peaks.

"There," she said, still pointing. "Don't you see them?"

"The mountains?"

"Yes, that is it. That is what they are called. I was just hoping that you could help me find what I am looking for, but I just can't seem to remember what it was that I lost!"

Thoughtfully thinking over my reply, I came up with a question that I hoped would jar her memory. "Did it have anything to do with a person?"

"Aha!" She clapped with excitement. I couldn't help but laugh at her. "That is it. I believe it did have something to do with a person. Do you know what it was?"

"I think I do," I admitted, but I didn't know how to tell her that I couldn't bring back what it was she had lost. "I just don't know if I can find what it is that you are looking for."

"I suppose you are right," she concluded. I could sense a feeling of compunction trapped within her saddening voice. "If I don't know what it is that I lost, then nobody will understand how to find it. None of us will understand," she told me, as she looked directly into my eyes. I could have sworn that I saw her soul come to life that very instant.

Yet, feeling despaired toward her circumstances, I wanted to do anything possible to help ease her mind and heart. So I asked her, "Would it help if I went up there to look for what it is that you lost?"

"Oh, I don't want to burden you, dear."

"Actually, Grandma, I think that it would be more of a burden on me to do nothing for you. I think that it is time to go back up there. Nobody has been up there for such a long time."

"Not since I lost what it is that I am searching for?" she asked.

"I think so. That is, if we are searching for the same thing," I determined.

"Oh, you are very sweet. It is so wonderful of you to offer to do this for me. It isn't easy for me to get around very much anymore."

"It is no problem."

"Now, one more thing before you go, dear. I was

wondering if you could find...what is that lady's name?" she pondered within her mind.

"Joan?" I suggested.

"Yes, that might be it. I was thinking Gail. You might be right, though."

"Grandma, I am Gail," I reminded her.

"Okay, honey. I just need her to help me find something. I lost something out there, and I can't remember what it was. Do you think that you can find her?"

"Yes, Grandma. I will find her for you. It is okay."

Chapter Twenty

Ring, ring! sounded the other end of the phone line. Finally, after five long and loud rings, the other end of the receiver was picked up.

"Hello?" sounded the sleepy voice.

"Hey, Damien. It is me. Were you napping?"

"Gail, where have you been? I've been worried sick about you! Why didn't you call us?"

"That is funny, because I was about to ask you about calling people you were supposed to call."

"What are you talking about?" he asked with annoyance.

"Don't get crabby with me," I ordered. "I am at Grandma Joan's place. She told me that you never called her about Grandpa's death. They didn't know anything about it. You lied to me. Right to my face. How could you do that?"

"Ah, Gail. I just didn't want to hurt you. You were so upset that day that I didn't want to make it worse. I never meant to lie to you. I just couldn't work up the nerve to call them. I was afraid that they wouldn't come. I'm sorry."

His voice sounded so sincere that I actually believed him. It was the fear that kept him from doing the one thing that his heart truly desired. Death and the fear surrounding us seemed to be the only thing that kept Damien and I attached.

"I'm sorry, too. I guess I could have called them myself, or we could have done it together instead of me leaving it solely up to you."

"Wow!" he exclaimed. "This is a change. I never thought that I would be around the day that you admitted you made a mistake."

"Shut up, I've been in the wrong several times. There is just no reason to dwell on it, so I don't see a reason for confessing the mistake."

"You are a piece of work," he bellowed. "So what are you doing? What took you so long to call us? Anneal is really upset."

"I'm sorry. It took so long, because I met somebody on the way up here. We just took a little detour."

"Well, who did you meet?"

"Actually, I ran into the same guy that helped Anneal and me save that deer."

"Oh, really?"

"Yes, and I don't want to hear any more from you about it."

"Well, get him to sleep with you so that we can hire him to work at the shelter," he joked.

"I'm working on it," I said, but quickly added, "The working at the shelter part, that is."

"Oh," he teased.

"So, where is Anneal? I wanted to talk to her. Is she there?"

"No, she called and said that she would be at the shelter until after six tonight. She wanted to work with the doe you brought in."

"How is the deer?"

"She is getting stronger every day. It is going to be a while before she is ready to be released. You should come home and see her for yourself," he suggested. "It might speed up her recovery. Her leg is still badly injured."

"I will. I'll be home soon, but I was actually hoping that you would come up here for a little bit." There was silence. Absolute silence. It was eventually followed by a deep sigh, but there weren't any words to follow the moaning whine. "Damien?"

"Gail, I was in the middle of a nap. Can you call back later and talk to Anneal?"

"You can't hide from them forever, Damien. I really think that it is time to forget the past."

"They are not very understanding people, Gail. They hated Grandpa for choosing us to live. Grandpa didn't have a choice. He did what Dad told him to do. They would have rather seen us die instead of their daughter."

"I don't think they meant it that way. They were just hurting in the same way we were."

"How can you defend them?"

"Damien, if you won't come for Tom or Joan, come for Grandma Mary. Mostly, come for me."

"Grandma Mary is the one who told us to never come back. And I won't come for you, because you are the one who can't let things go. You never give up until you have the last say in something. You can't tell me that you are even close to feeling happy about going back to see them." he shouted through the phone. His voice was so loud that I had to pull the receiver away from my ear.

"I guess I'll call you later, but I don't know when. I was going to head up the mountain tomorrow."

"You're what!?"

"Damien, I'm tired of waiting around. Everyone is being ridiculous. Mom and Dad are up there all alone. I'm going to see them tomorrow."

"You can't go alone! What did Joan and Tom say? What about Grandma Mary?"

"They don't know yet. You don't care what they think anyway. And since I can't let things go, Caden has agreed to go with me tomorrow."

"Gail, I forbid you to go."

"I'm going. If you want to stop me, you have to come get me."

"Gail?"

Diary: A new beginning

19 June 03

Why is it that we as human beings always expect the worst? Is it because we are afraid to discover the truth? Has everything always turned out so horrible in our lives that we find it absolutely necessary to prepare ourselves for the bad news before we even receive it?

At some point in our life, we will all have to live up to our fears. There is a mystery behind all our hidden trepidation that is finally solved when we unravel the conundrum puzzling our inner being. Once we understand why our apprehension weighs us down, we will be able to take flight in life and soar to new heights. Yet, the first step taken to find our cowering courage is the most difficult to reach. Still, until we lift both feet off the ground, we will never land with dignity and grace.

Chapter Twenty-One

"What are you writing about?" curious Caden inquisitively questioned, as he plopped down next to me on the porch swing. Unlike most porch swings, this one was positioned to face the outside world. It wasn't directly centered toward the house itself. Instead, it hung steadily to swing our minds into the world beyond. Even the porch's white railing could not keep it caged. It had been removed long ago in order to free us from the captivity of the bustling life surrounding the family.

Placing the diary off to my side, I casually turned and asked, "What do you see out there?"

"Ah, I see a barn with cows grazing before it."

"Not there," I said rolling my eyes. "Farther out there."

"I know what you meant," he said laughing. "What I see are mountains, but that isn't what you see, is it?"

Caden always knew what Gail was thinking. She didn't

know how he knew, but she was glad that he did. Sometimes she thought it was because they had seen things that most people never have to worry about experiencing. Then, there were times that she would just sit back and convince herself that they were just meant to be together. Little did they know, their stories were just beginning to merge as one.

"When I look out there, I see an end to a beginning. It is an ending that should have been written long ago, but my fear kept me from seeing that," I explained to him.

"I'm glad it did, because if it hadn't stopped you, we might not have ever met."

Unfortunately, he was right. If I had decided to stay with my grandparents, our story together would be completely different. We may not have even had a story together, or would we? It really made me wonder if we really were meant to be together forever.

"Why does life have to be so complicated?" I asked him, but he couldn't answer. He just looked at me and shook his head back and forth. "Perhaps we just aren't ready to know why life occurs the way it does."

"Dinner is ready!" Joan shouted from the doorway. "Oh, there you are. Have you seen your grandfather, Gail?" she asked me once she had seen us gliding gently back and forth upon the swing.

"No, but I wanted to ask you something anyway," I told her.

"Oh, what is it?"

"It is about Grandma Mary."

"Honey, I told you not to get your hopes up."

"It isn't that," I informed her. "She asked about something she had lost in the mountains. She told me that it had to do with a person. I thought that it was my dad, but I'm not so sure. Surely, she would remember losing her son the way she did."

"Well, her mind is slipping. She may not remember. I think that it is better that she doesn't remember. She doesn't have to hurt anymore," Joan remarked, but the tone of her voice told me something different. Due to her nervousness, it was obvious that she had been hiding something.

"What is going on? I heard dinner was ready, so I came up here to eat. All I see is the three of you staring each other down," Tom stated, as he stepped upon the porch.

"We were just discussing Grandma Mary," I told him.

"That old coot? Her mind is so far out there that half the time she doesn't even know her own name. Of course, she does seem much happier now that she doesn't have to think about her son and the fact that she chased off her only two grandchildren," Tom commented, with a wave of his hand. He acted as he could care less if she died that very moment.

"Wow," Caden remarked, "you have no idea what it is like to watch someone die. I hope to God that you never do, but it sure would change your life's perspective real quick."

"You have no business talking to me like that in my own house!" Tom shouted. "You are a guest in this house. You better learn to mind your own business real fast, son. You know nothing of death!"

"I know what death is. I lost my baby girl!" Joan shouted.

I hated to see them fight. I was beginning to think that Damien was right. Maybe it was a mistake to go back, but it was too late to think so narrow-mindedly.

"What in the world is wrong with you people!" I shouted in anger, as I jumped off the swing and landed perfectly with both feet on the ground. "For the past twenty years I have been trying to convince myself that there was nothing to fear about this place. I finally worked up the nerve to come back here and face my past, and it is starting all over again.

"The day we left to go climbing, you got into a fight with your daughter. You told her that the mountain was not safe because of the rains. Everyone disagreed with you, and we decided to go anyway. But you didn't want to go. Well, as we all know, you were right. Well, congratulations! Now get over it! Did you hate your daughter that much for disagreeing with you? Did you hate her that much that you don't want to remember her? Did you?"

"What about you? You never came back here until now!" Joan screamed.

"You left us behind!" Tom shouted in agreement with Joan.

"I left you behind because you couldn't look Damien and me in the eye after they died. Grandma Mary told us to never come back. I used to think that each of you wanted Damien and me to die instead of Mom and Dad. Screw the grandchildren! Mom and Dad could have reproduced!" I screamed in accusation. "But that wasn't it, was it?" I said, as I rethought my position. "Mary couldn't leave because she kept waiting for them to come back. Yet, deep inside, she knew they would never be seen again. She blamed Noah, but she was there. She knew she could have tried to help them, but she didn't.

"And you, the two of you, you blamed Noah because he was the leader. It hurt to think that you could have stopped us from going if you really wanted to. You could have gone, and maybe you could have helped us. But you didn't!

"The truth of the matter is that all of us made decisions that day that we can't change. What we have to do now is wonder if it really would have made a difference. None of us could have prevented that mudslide. Who knows, maybe if you had come, you would be dead, too. We can't change the past, but we can change our future for the better if we only believe that we can make it right. We have to stop forgetting and remember the sacrifice they made so that we could live."

"It isn't true," Joan cried, disputing my reasoning of their hatred toward Noah and their own daughter for disobeying them. "We didn't hate her. We were angry when she went, and we did think that we could have helped if we went. We wanted to blame everyone but ourselves. So we did blame Noah, but mostly we blamed you."

"What?" I asked, as my heart sank. I felt a lump forming in my throat, but I couldn't swallow it. I didn't want the tears to escape, and as long as I choked on the lump in my throat, I could manage to maintain control of my emotions.

"We told ourselves that if you hadn't run out to save them and gotten in the way, they could have been helped," Tom answered. "Then we convinced Mary of the same. We told her that if the two of you chose to go with Noah, then you were choosing to live with a murderer, and you were accessories to the crime," he cried. "And we wondered why you never came to visit us. I'm so sorry," he sobbed.

"I don't believe this. I spent years trying to convince myself that what I thought wasn't the truth, but it turns out that I was right."

"We are sorry," Joan cried in pain.

"You are sorry!" I yelled. "Every day of my life, for the past twenty years, I have had to live with this scar on my hand! Plus, deal with the death of my parents on top of that, and all you can say is sorry?"

"We don't know what else to say," Joan said.

"What do you want us to do?" Tom asked.

I didn't know how to answer. All I wanted to do was find the truth. I never thought about what I would say when I heard it. I never even imagined what I would do if all my paranoid delusions became reality.

"Maybe we should go," Caden suggested.

"No, I don't want to go. I came all this way. I'm not leaving," I said. "Only, I don't know what to do now. I don't know what to say."

Tom, stepped forward and said, "We completely understand if you want to go."

"No. I thought that I had it bad, but the three of you have had it so much worse. I felt bad for isolating you, but you isolated yourselves. I just don't know what to say. Did you really believe that I killed them?"

"No, of course not. You missed the point. We had to, because we truly blamed ourselves for letting all of you go that day," Tom replied.

"You know, everyone around me tried to forget what happened. I am the only one, besides Noah, who tried to remember everything. My problem was that I thought about it too much. Well, at least I know where I came from, and now I am trying to figure out where I am going, but I will always know who I am. I am..."

Interrupting, Joan said, "Honey, don't say it. You are not a murderer."

"I wasn't going to say that," I said in disbelief. "But I was going to say that I am the daughter of two loving souls. Souls who died to save me. The rest of you are going to have to admit that to yourselves, or you are going to waste away to less than Mary has."

"Is that what you want us to do? You want us to believe that they were sacrificed so that you could live?" Tom asked.

"I'm asking you to believe there was a reason. I'm not telling you it was only for me, because I think there is more to it than that. We might not ever know, but at least I am willing to remember the sacrifice," I stated, and quickly turned toward the house. The hatred trapped inside of them was beginning to filter through my own soul, and I could not allow myself to stand still and let it happen.

"Wait!" Joan pleaded. "I know what Mary searches for!" she called to me, as I began to walk back into the house, but I never turned to listen. I suppose I was frightened to hear the secret, but it wasn't the fear of the hidden truth this time. It was the fear of hate, the hate that was beginning to brew inside my veins. It was the fear of hating my family once again.

Caden, on the other hand, had followed me to the door, but he stopped to hear the hidden secret. He was the type who had to know. He had to know every little detail, because piecing them together was what kept his mind in circulation.

"What is it that Gail needed to know? What have you hidden from her now?" he asked.

"There was a necklace," Joan sobbed. "Noah sent it to Mary on her birthday one year. Each year after that he sent a new picture of the children. She always kept it close to her heart. One day I took it from her. I wanted her to let the children go just like the way we forgot the rest of them, so I buried it. I buried it just before the path that leads to the mountains. Gail will know what I am talking about," Joan explained with sorrow. "Let her know that I didn't mean to hurt anyone."

"There have been several times that you have never meant to hurt anyone, but it is obvious that each of your choices has not been for the better. How could you take a dying woman's heart?" Caden asked.

"Son," Tom replied, "as I said before, you know nothing of death. You don't know what it is like to lose almost your entire family. All you want to do is forget it. If you don't, you feel that you will die right along with them. All we wanted was some dignity in our life and their death.

Someday you will understand that, but I hope that it does not have to be the way in which we have learned."

"I know death, sir. I look at the scars of it each morning in the mirror," he said, as he pointed to the scars on his face. "I know what it is like to watch someone die. It is something that the mind never forgets but learns to understand.

"Don't watch your life fade from your very own eyes. We all die in this life one way or another, but we do not have to let our lives slip away before they are officially gone. And what you need to understand is that there is never any dignity in death, but there is always meaning. The meaning of death comes from the way our mind perceives the purpose of it. Do you believe that your daughter's death came without meaning?"

"No, not at all," they said together.

"Then stop pretending it never happened. Then, maybe you can bring some dignity back into your life."

Chapter Twenty-Two

"What did she mean that she buried it at the beginning of the path?" Caden softly asked, as we hiked our way through the woods outside of Tom and Joan's farmhouse.

Most of the walk the following morning had been hiked in silence. Caden could tell I wasn't in the mood for conversing, but that one question just seemed to jump from the tip of his tongue. It was a simple question that warranted an easy answer, but all of the jumbling thoughts that seemed to stupefy my mind kept me from offering a fair answer.

"Gail?" he called again. "Hello?"

Shrugging my shoulders, I rumbled, "I don't know, all right. They are idiots!"

"Hey, hey! Take it easy. I'm not the bad guy here."

"I know. I'm sorry. Just...how could they do that? Why would you take away the only thing that an old woman felt that she had left? They didn't have any right to do that," I said out of breath. My puffing lungs eventually gasped, "I need to rest. I thought I was in good shape from working at the camp, but I guess I was wrong."

"You should try hitchhiking," Caden joked. "It will get your heart pumping every time."

"Ha, ha," I said, as I collapsed upon a fallen tree trunk. "Man, I don't remember this walk taking this long as a child."

"I think that you have gotten yourself so worked up about your grandparents that you just can't get seem to get yourself calmed back down. Not to mention, you are probably anxious about going back to a place that you have feared since you were six."

"You are probably right. I mean, I know you are right," I pointed out. "But I shouldn't take my frustration out on you. Thank you for staying with me."

"I would never let you go up here alone," he told me again.

"Thanks, but that isn't really what I meant. I meant thanks for coming to my grandparents' place with me. I almost left without you. I really don't think that I would have made it this far without you. The minute I heard how much blame they placed on me and the rest of the family, I was ready to walk away from this place again, but then I overheard what you said to my grandfather," I explained to Caden. His head turned away from mine and began to look over the distant hills smothered in forestland. "Thank you for what you said and for helping me figure out what Mary has lost."

"I only agreed with what you have been trying to say to everyone, but I do think you are wrong about one thing," he remarked, as his head turned back to face me. He searched my eyes for only a moment until he said, "You are wrong about Mary. She only thought she had lost you, but you never left here. This place has always been on your mind, and you have always been on her mind. Though the memories have been dark, they have still always been a part of you. The ones that have lost you are the ones that cast you into the shadows of their minds long ago."

"I'm so glad that I met you," I whispered loudly, for only him to hear.

"I'm so glad that you taught me not to hide from myself," he whispered back.

"C'mon, suddenly I feel very refreshed."

With each step approaching the path to my past, my mind worried that it would be difficult to see the present with truth and understanding. Yet my heart pressed forward once again, while reminding me that it would be even more difficult to turn back at that point. Somehow, deep within my soul's existence, I knew that everything was going to be all right. There was nothing to fear, except a future without the hope that circumambulates forward from the past in order to help us become who we believe ourselves to be.

"Is this it? Is this where it happened?"

"No, Caden," I replied, as we stood staring at the tombstones directly before us. "This is where their bodies were found. The accident happened up there," I said, pointing to the ledge jutting out from the rock's edge.

"That is a long way up."

Stepping off the path that separated us from the mountain, I stated, "Yes, it is."

"Do you want me to give you a moment?" he asked, without following me.

"Please," I spoke aloud in a delicate tone, a tone that could not stir or waken the dead's past.

Caressing the top of the grave's cold stone, the muscles in

my hands tensed. The feel of the crumbling rock between my fingers brought dripping tears to my eyes.

Alone they lay, so cold and alone. No one even bothered to visit once. We just let their deaths crumble our lives. Even their names could no longer be read.

"I am sorry that we let this happen. Not your deaths. We could not prevent that. I know that now, but we could have prevented you from dying during your eternal rest. Your headstone shatters within the palms of my scarred hands, and the weeds thrive within the decaying soil beneath my feet. How my heart mourns and, at the same time, shudders in the joy it receives from speaking to you. For it is by the grace of God's hand that the life around you is beginning to bloom once again."

Drying her eyes with the bottom of her shirt, she turned to Caden as she rose from her knees. His eyes did not weep at the sight of a child kneeling in remorse but at how she sparkled as a woman when she walked away from the graves that day.

"Their graves are in ruins. I am sorry," he said.

"I'm not. Their spirits are free, and that is what is important. The graves can be replaced."

"What about the necklace? Can it be replaced for your grandmother?"

"No, but she can have me if we cannot find it on our way back down."

"You mean on our way home?"

The world around us seemed to disappear the farther we climbed, and the time passed by without a care. I'm not sure whether it was because I could not wait to view the world from the top ledge once again, or if it was because we really did take our time to reach the top, but one thing that I do know for sure is that we were not frightened. In actuality, neither of us wanted the moment to come to an end. It was a splendiferous moment that seemed to be filled with absolute glory within itself.

"You know, my memories of this place may have once been filled with darkened gloom, but it is so different now. I see nothing but light."

"Isn't it odd how we see what we feel?" Caden asked.

The pale, sticky smog that once plagued the atmosphere had dispersed and been replaced by the light of the sun. Emerging crests of clouds swirled about the cerulean sky until they gathered in achromatic puffs of cottony white.

Even a choir of harmonious birds could be heard chirping upon the branches of the white pines below us. Their soulful tune of praise could be heard echoing throughout the valley of life.

"I just pray for my grandmother's sake that we find the locket. I just don't know where exactly to look along the path," I said to Caden.

"I guess we could look for loose soil."

"Yeah, but how long ago did she bury it?"

"True. She could have been a little clearer on where it was buried. What we need is a sign from above."

As soon as Caden spoke those words, a miraculous scene occurred. Some might believe that it was only a mere coincidence or that we fooled ourselves into believing it was a sign from a higher power. For me, too many pieces of the puzzle were beginning to fit together.

"Whoa, look at that!" exclaimed Caden. "It looks like her. It looks like the eagle I rescued. Doesn't it?"

The brown and white bird swooped about the edge of the cliff. With a flap and a flutter of her wings, the acrobat soared into the sky as she looped, whirled, and twirled her way through the clouds. Her eagle eye caught a glimpse of

The Woodcarver's Hand

its prey upon the ground beneath her. Without warning, she dove. She dove so far and so fast that we thought she would crash, so we flung ourselves upon the ground in order to peer over the ledge. Our hands gripped tighter and tighter into the edge of the cliff the closer the eagle came to the ground. Suddenly, just before crashing, she pulled up her head and snatched her prey between her claws. When she was certain she had a tight grip upon the victim, she released the loose debris from her death clutch. It fell and fell until it smashed upon the earth's crust.

"Ouch!" I cried out in pain.

"Yeah, good thing nobody was below there," Caden concluded.

"No, my hand. My scar is bleeding!"

"From what?"

"I don't know. I think I reopened the wound on the edge of the cliff," I whimpered, as I sat upon my knees and cradled my hand within the other one.

"Let me see it," Caden ordered, as he grabbed my hands. He held them out in front of him until the sun's light shined upon them. "It doesn't look that bad. It is just a little scratch over top of your scar. It's fine," he said, as if I were overreacting.

Of course, he was right, but it wasn't the blood or the scratch that had frightened me. The idea of my scar changing its appearance is what startled me the most. After staring at it for nearly 20 years, I had become accustomed to its disfigured features. At that particular moment, after finally gaining the strength to face my worst nightmare, I would have to learn to adapt to the new change. Not only the change of accepting the loss of my parents, but dealing with the new features in the life surrounding me; and in return, this change included any new scars that came along with the adaptation.

"Mom! Dad! Hold on! I won't let you go!"

"You have to, honey. It is your only chance of survival!"

"But I can't do it, Dad! I don't think that I can live without you! Please, don't leave me behind! We have so much left to do. Please, don't let go. Don't give up hope! Hang on! I will fight for you!"

"Just look over the edge and let go! It will be all right! You will see. Let go of our hands, baby girl. We will always be with you."

"But Mom! I love you. I never told you that, but I do love you. I didn't mean to get in the way. I would have never purposely let you fall. You know that, right?"

"We know that! It is time!"

"I'll never forget you!"

With those words, Gail's hand released its grip on the life she had once known.

"Gail!" called a voice from the outside world. "Gail! Are you all right?"

"Huh?" I sounded with confusion. My mind felt as if it had been living in a delusion of life. It was as though I had been a prisoner trapped inside another world and had just discovered a way out.

"You just blacked out, and you kept getting closer to the edge. For a minute, I thought you were going to jump. It was like you believed you could fly."

"No, I'm just learning to fly," I declared.

"I know just what you mean," he said in return. "Did you find what you were looking for?"

"Almost everything," I replied. "I just need to find an old woman's heart."

"Maybe we just need to know where to look," Caden said, as he stepped closer to the edge of the cliff and peered over the edge. "It is somewhere down there, right?"

"Yes," I said. "Somewhere on the path we stepped off of before we came up here. I didn't see anything on the way up here, though."

"Maybe it was because we weren't looking from the right perspective."

"What do you mean?"

Motioning for me to step closer to the edge, he said, "Look just before the path at the foot of the hill."

Cautiously finding my footing, I took hold of his hand and peered over the edge. To my surprise, I saw something new for the first time. If I hadn't made the climb to the top, it would have been impossible for me to see what was just beneath us.

"It is a cross!" I exclaimed.

"And it is made out of stones," Caden remarked. "A person could only see it if they were looking down upon it."

"She must have buried it the way she did so that my parents could look down upon the locket and not feel alone."

"Or because she felt that their hearts had been buried along with your parents, and the only way they could be saved was by the Lord."

"I guess we'll never know," I told him in exchange for reason. "And I'll never ask her why she buried it there. Maybe she needs to figure that out on her own."

Chapter Twenty-Three

"Who is at your grandparents' place?" Caden wondered, as we hiked our way back from the mountains.

"This is something I never thought that I would see," I stated. "I can't believe he actually showed up."

With the locket around my neck, we quickened our pace toward the house. I wasn't overcome with joy to see my brother's truck in the driveway, but I was interested in why he had decided to come after all. I prayed it wasn't to lecture me about my past choices.

Stepping through the door, Caden and I were greeted with silence. With a quick glance of dread directed at each other, we continued to make our way through the house and into the living room. Many times I had pictured a family reunion, and it never ended euphorically. So as we made our presence known, I half expected to find somebody missing or a body hidden in a closet.

"Hi. You guys made it," I said to Damien and Anneal. "How are you doing?" I asked, looking about the room. Their eyes never moved from Caden. I could almost see the daggers shooting into his heart, which wasn't much different from what I imagined. Only, I pictured the daggers heading in my direction and Caden catching one for being a bystander.

"Hi, Gail," Anneal said, as she rushed to my side and hugged me tightly. "I'm so glad that you are all right. I have been very worried about you," she said, and turned in Caden's direction. "So, hopefully you have learned his name by now."

"Oh, yeah," I said with embarrassment for not introducing everyone. "His name is Caden."

"Just Caden, huh?" she questioned, firmly shaking his hand.

Shaking her hand in return, he said, "Well, my full name is John Caden Evert, but I prefer Caden. It is an unusual name, so it fits me better."

"I'll say," Damien said quietly, as a side note.

"Don't mind him," Anneal ordered. "You know you saved that deer's life, and she is doing better every day. Hopefully, we will be able to release her soon. I'm not so sure about her injured leg, though. She doesn't want to put her weight on it and keeps hobbling around. But even if we do release her, we are reluctant to let her go back in the cemetery. We are concerned for her safety, as well as the cemetery's landscape. The only problem is that her daughter is still roaming there. We've spotted her several times," she explained. I could tell she was looking for some input from Caden.

"Um, you could capture the fawn and release them in a safer environment together," Caden happily responded.

"We have thought about that, but with the minimum staff we have, it will be difficult to spare someone," Damien said, as he shot me a look of abandonment.

"I'm about ready to return home," I immaturely told him. "There are just some things that I need to do first."

"You have been gone for nearly three weeks. I'm sure that everything you needed to do is taken care of by now." He scowled. "I think that it is time for you to come home. The kids at the camp think that you have abandoned them."

"The kids or you? The kids understand a lot more than you think. Sometimes I think that they understand more than you," I respectfully implied.

"What does that mean?" he asked in a snippy manner. "All you think about is yourself. Whatever you feel makes you happy, you do without regard to anyone else."

"Okay, that is enough," Anneal scolded. "What is the matter with you?" she snapped, but it wasn't at me like I had expected. "She is here because she thinks of everyone but herself. Have you not been listening to your sister? She left because she couldn't handle herself around the children after Noah's death. She needed to get away and find herself again. The only way that she could do that was by coming back to the one place that both of you have ignored since you were kids. Please, give her a little credit and respect. I trust her implicitly. Every decision she has made is for the better. When she is ready to come home, I'll be waiting for her."

"Thank you, Anneal," I said gratefully. "Unfortunately, though, when I left, I think I was more concerned with myself, but everything I have seen and done in the past few weeks has changed my perspective."

"I have to disagree," Caden altercated with passion. "I think you had every intention of bettering yourself, as well as the others around you. If you never believed in anyone else but yourself, then you wouldn't be standing here this very moment trying to convince everyone that their lives have a purpose and that your parents aren't lost to any of you."

I was eternally obliged to know that he always believed I had been proceeding with amelioration. My only regret during that moment was that he could not see how much he had helped me achieve.

"Wow," Anneal sounded. "Why can't I find a man like that?"

"Hey," Damien argued. "Gail, can I please talk to you in private for a moment?"

"Yeah, that's fine. If it makes you more comfortable," I said, as I glanced at the reactions of everyone in the room. I was concerned that Joan and Tom would be hurt by Damien's reaction to the entire situation, but they had yet to even account for my presence. Since I had walked into the room, I hadn't even seen them look in my direction.

"Look, I'm sorry that I came off a little strongly, but I am not comfortable here at all."

"What did you say to them, Damien? They haven't acknowledged one word that we have said since we have been back. What is going on?"

"I told them that I was going to tell you what they had said to me the day after Mom and Dad's funeral."

"What are you talking about? They already told me that they blamed Noah and mostly me for the accident," I informed him.

"And you are okay with that?"

"Well no, but they know they were wrong. They felt bad about not being there. They felt that if they were there, they might have been able to do something to help. They were just upset and angry about the entire situation. We all were."

"I never told you that they blamed you, because I didn't

think that you could handle it."

"So you knew? Is that why you kept me away from here for so long?"

"After the funeral, they tried to convince me that you and Grandpa were murderers and that I should stay away from you."

"They said it like that?"

"Not exactly. They just said that it was your fault that Mom and Dad were dead. Grandma Mary told them what had happened. She said that if Grandpa didn't have to save you, then Mom and Dad would have had a fighting chance. Grandpa wouldn't have had to make a decision about who would live and who would die."

"So, you stood up for me, right?"

"Well, yeah. You are my little sister. You were only six. All you wanted to do was save them like the rest of us."

"You should have told me this before now. My whole life I thought that you were just being ignorant, and I hated you for not letting me make my own decisions."

"I just hated to see you blame yourself for their death. I thought that if you came back here and heard what they were saying, you would actually believe you were a murderer. I couldn't let you do that. That is why I never called them about Grandpa's funeral. I thought that if they even came, they would be happy about his death. I just didn't want to see you get hurt, but in the process of protecting you, I hurt you. I'm sorry."

"Damien?" I called to him. His head was bowed low to the floor.

"Yeah," he said, shuffling his feet.

"Thanks for being my brother," I said with a hug.

Peeking her head through the doorframe, Anneal said with a tease, "Ah, how cute."

"Oh, shut up," Damien joked and kissed her lips. "Come on, let's get out of here."

"Oh, wait. I have something for Mary," I said, revealing the locket around my neck.

"That belonged to Mom!" Damien exclaimed. "Dad bought it to give to her on her birthday, but they died before they had a chance to celebrate it. Where did you get it?"

"Joan said that Grandpa gave it to Mary on her birthday. It was the year Mom and Dad died."

"Your dad was so proud of that locket," Joan called from the living room. "He showed it to us. It had your baby pictures in it, and he had the back labeled 'opportunity.' They loved the town of Opportunity, because it was where they met, got married, began their careers, and had the two of you. They said the town's name told you everything you needed to know about the place. He just couldn't wait to give it to her."

"So when they died, Noah decided to give it to Mary," I concluded. "He hoped it would help her be reminded of her family."

"Yes, which was why I took it and buried it. I just wanted to forget about everything that happened. Every time I looked at her wearing that necklace, I couldn't help but think of them. I wanted to bury it with them, but I just couldn't work up the courage to face them. My feet just wouldn't move off that path. So I buried it in a way that they would always be able to see it. I thought it was only fair to leave it with them. I never thought it would trouble Mary so much; she has such a bad memory."

"Joan?" I called, as she began to cry uncontrollably.

"Please, call us Grandma and Grandpa. We do miss it," Tom stated.

"Grandma," I said with a smile. I hated to see her

suffering in her own guilt. "Did Grandpa Noah know about Mary's condition?"

"He knew she was getting sick before the accident. Once she lost her family, she just seemed to get worse year by year. Noah never knew how bad she was. In a way, I think it was better. He wrote her so many beautiful letters. If he had known about her condition, then things wouldn't have been the same for her. She may have gotten worse sooner," Grandma Joan explained.

"What is the matter with her?" Damien asked.

"Would you like to come with me and give this back to her?" I asked him. "She is just upstairs in her room."

On our way upstairs, I tried as much as possible to explain the state of Grandma Mary's condition to Damien. He never grasped the seriousness of the situation until we opened the door leading to her room. He made several attempts to gain her attention, but with each spoken word, she continued to stare out to the mountains.

Finally making my presence known to her, I held out my hand before me until she grasped it in her own. Smiling at her, I said, "It is me, Gail. Grandma, do you remember me? We spoke this morning about something you had lost."

"I'm not sure, but I do remember that I had lost something. So I guess I do remember speaking to you. Did you find what it was that I had lost?"

"I think so. I found this out by the mountains," I said, as I showed her the locket cupped within the opposite hand she held. "It was right where you said it was."

"Oh, it is beautiful," she said, as she took the locket into her hands. With a bright smile, she held it up in the light of the windows for a better glimpse. "I think you found my heart."

"Open it up," I told her.

"Huh," she gasped, "look at these children. Are they mine? They look like someone I remember. Did you know them?"

"Grandma, those are your grandchildren. That one is your granddaughter, Gail, and this one here is your grandson, Damien."

"They sound so familiar. I wish I could find them," she sobbed. "I don't think they like me very much if they don't come to see me."

"No, they do like you," Damien replied. "They just couldn't remember how much they liked you until now."

"You are a very nice young man. What is your name again?"

"Damien. Grandma, I am Damien."

"Of course you are," she said. "Do you think you could get me some water? I am very thirsty."

"Yes, Grandma," Damien responded. "I will get you some water. I will be right back," he said. I could feel his heart shatter as he walked away from the room. It was much like the way mine felt the first time I had spoken to her.

"Grandma, I will be right back," I informed her. "I promise."

"Well, all right then, Gail. As long as you promise you will come back, you may go."

"Grandma?" I turned in shock just as I was leaving the room.

"Please, turn out the lights on your way out, dear. I am feeling a little tired."

"Sure, Grandma. I'll see you."

"Just don't stay away for too long. I get awfully lonely."

Chapter Twenty-Four

"Are you sure you won't come?"

"I can't. It just isn't my place, but I will be around."

"I'm really going to miss you, Caden."

"Not as much as I am going to miss you. I never thought that I would love anyone again the way I love you. I guess I was wrong."

"Each time we meet someone, we learn new ways to love them. Love is never the same twice. Sometimes when we find someone again, the connection of love between them grows even stronger."

"But when we meet again, I don't want to love you in any other way. My heart is inflamed with so much passion for you now that I don't think it can handle any more."

Wow, Gail! You must be an idiot, leaving this man behind. Don't do it. Stay with him!

"Oh, Caden, you have no idea how many women want a

man to say a line like that about them, but I don't think that we can do this right now," I said to him, and watched the hopeful expression upon his face drop and fall into the dust beneath his feet. I was positive that he was waiting for me to trample upon it next. "It just goes back to what we talked about before. How can we begin a new relationship when we haven't got the ones already in our lives straightened out? What are we supposed to do?"

"I think that your family is beginning to come back together. You and your brother have made arrangements to get together with your grandparents once a month so that you can visit your parents' graves. And your grandmother Mary is at least recognizing you sometimes now. All you have to do is keep trying to repair your relationship with your brother and Anneal. I'm sure the rec center and the animal shelter will run fine without you for a while."

"And what am I supposed to do? I can't just pack everything up and leave them hanging back home. We are in the middle of trying to put our lives back together. The rec center and animal shelter are falling apart. I can't stay here with you," I informed him, as we climbed out of the jeep together. It was only seconds later when Malachi appeared on the front porch. He smiled and waved as if he knew it was us the moment we had pulled into the driveway.

"What I am supposed to do?" Caden countered, as we flung ourselves on top of the jeep's front hood. Like children, we rocked our legs back and forth in unison until the pattern was broken by Caden's clashing leg. With one sideways lunge, he broke the rhythm between us. "I can't just leave him here all alone. The guy can barely get around anymore. Look at him."

On the front porch, Malachi struggled to find his way toward the porch steps. With each forward step he took, his walking stick kept striking an object within his path. Every time he turned to search for a clearer walkway, he found himself trapped.

"Caden, sometimes I think that man sees more clearly than the rest of the world put together. He does have difficulty getting around at times, but if you gave the man some room to move he would probably be just fine.

"But I do know how you feel about him, and you do owe him a lot. If you think this is where you belong, then you should stay here and take care of things," I said, as I leaned my head upon his shoulder.

Supporting my weight in his arms, he leaned our bodies back across the top of the hood until we could rest easily upon the windshield. Taking my left hand within his own, he wrapped his fingers tightly around mine and said, "Just relax and listen."

"For what?" I asked him.

"Just listen," he said, as he placed my right hand upon his heart. Then he did the same by placing his right hand upon my heart and said, "Just listen to my words and hear the air in my lungs breathe. Feel how my heart beats just for you when you are near. No matter how far apart we are, you could never be too far away for me to feel you inside my soul."

With every breath he took, I felt my lungs deepen to breathe the same air he breathed. By his heart, I felt the blood in my own veins thrive. In our hands, our lives began to fade into one.

Chapter Twenty-Five

"I think this is the best idea that you have ever had!"

"Why thank you, Damien. How could you have ever doubted me?"

"It will never happen again!" he stated, as he flung his arm around my shoulders and gently bumped my hip with his own. "The kids love this! I love this!"

"The parents love it, too!" Anneal proclaimed. She had been giving a tour to the camp's regular attending families. The parents seemed thrilled about the new additions at the recreation center. "I think by combining the camp with the animal shelter, we are making the environment therapeutic for the children and animals."

"Yeah, they seem to be loving it," I agreed, without much emotion. I really hadn't heard much of what she had said. I had been too busy watching the children feed a young and familiar doe.

"Gail, I am sorry we couldn't do anything else for her," Anneal said, referring to the doe Caden and I had rescued.

After a few months, we finally realized that if we released the doe, her chances of survival were slim. The bone in her leg would never heal properly enough to allow her to walk or run well enough to survive in the wild. Even if a predator didn't pick her off, chances are she would starve to death.

Anneal was positive that she would have to put the doe down, so naturally I fought to save her. She became the inspiration for "The Lantern of Noah's Ark," the merging of the "Noah's Ark" and "The Lantern." I figured each group of children would greatly benefit by having their own animal to care for and nurture. Plus, each of the injured animals would heal quicker by receiving the love from a child's heart. The animals that could never be released would have a home for life.

"It is better than the alternative," I finally said to Anneal. "And since we were able to find and relocate her fawn, whether they know it or not, they will be able to see each other every day. The nearest source of water for the fawn is the camp's pond. When it is quiet, and nobody is looking, she'll do what she needs to survive. She'll be just fine," I explained, and added, "Plus, this way I know they are both doing well."

"Her daughter is very strong," Damien announced. "She will make it without her. I too have a feeling she is going to be just fine."

"And her mother will be as long as we can find somebody to help Anneal take care of the animals," I said.

"She'll be fine even if we don't," Anneal disputed. "As long as we don't take in any new animals until we find someone, we will be fine. I'm just glad we didn't have to shut completely down after Noah's death."

"You mean after Dr. Temper ran out on us," Damien argued.

"Oh, he was never very happy with the shelter. Noah didn't pay him much at all. He couldn't afford to. The only reason he agreed to help Noah out after Dad's death was because he had been Noah's best friend since they were kids. He knew it was Noah's dream and couldn't stand to see him shut it down," I justified. "Things are going to be just fine."

"I agree. I mean, where else can a girl hang out with her best friend and her boyfriend while doing what she loves to do?" Anneal inquired with a smile.

"You mean, where can a girl find the most ways to be annoying?" Damien joked.

"I think you are both wrong," I interjected. "I think what you mean to say is that this is the best place a person can learn about themselves. They are surrounded by everyone who loves them most. Everywhere they look, they can find someone who is willing to help them through every challenge placed before. But most of all, during their time spent here, they will be able to understand how much beauty thrives in the world. And they owe it all to the woodcarver's hand."

Diary: self-identity assessment

1 July 03

Matthew 6:25-27:
   "Therefore I tell you, do not worry about your life, what you will eat or drink; or about your body, what you will wear. Is not life more important than food, and the body more important than clothes? Look at the birds of the air; they do not sow or reap or store away in barns, and yet your heavenly father feeds them. Are you not much more valuable than they are? Who of you by worrying can add a single

hour to his life?"

When we wake each morning and stare into the mirror before us, do we always like what we see? Of course not, we are only human. Maybe it is our ratty hair or our mangled clothes or perhaps even our body itself that we find unattractive. But why worry about the vehicle that transports the soul?

If you flipped yourself inside out, would you then like the image you see? Would you see yourself the way you believe yourself to be or the way you desire yourself to be? If you aren't who you see yourself as in life, would it be time for a change? And if you decided to change your heart into your soul's most desired passion, would it be the correct choice? Perhaps not, but then again, you may be on your way to developing the character you were written to become.

Basically, we'll never know if we can become the character we most desire to be until we take the first step. So why not begin now?

It seems that it took me a lifetime to understand these words myself, but eventually I came to learn that it is up to me to decide if I really want to lead the life I was born to live. My character may have been carved out and my destiny written, but the decisions in my life are not made for me. So I may stumble and fall along the way, but I have the ability to start again. At any time in my life, I can choose to follow a different path, but no matter where it may lead me, I know that my creator will never give up on me. He will never stop searching for a way into my heart. Even on my judgment day, I know I will feel him ever present. But I fear it will be too late for some souls. If a soul never knew his creator, would he be allowed to open the door to heaven? Would you let a stranger into your home?

The Eyes of an Eagle

*Time,
it passes and fades.
With an absent mind as a guide,
it shows no mercy to the lost.*

*Skies of dark will turn to cotton candy clouds of beauty
that will give rise to royal blue blankets of canvass
that will begin to paint this marble blue planet of wonder,
while sunset fires reflect from ocean crests
and become engulfed by the endless sea.*

*Faces begin to fade and are swept away by
yesterdays
that turn to morrows,
while we are left to wonder
where life ran away to
before
flying away in search of
strength
and wisdom through the eyes of an eagle*

Wings of time beat to the rhythm found inside one's soul. Dance to the beat of your life, and ride alert upon the spirit soaring high above it all. And within your heart, you will see that you can soar high enough to shake hands with the stars set aside to shine bright for you alone.

The distance traveled to find the truth in the light shining in your heart reveals the limits you set for yourself. The path chosen to abide by demonstrates your abilities to endure obstacles placed upon the path you choose to find your destiny.

In the end, surviving the test of time is given to us the moment we enter the world. Through the events in our lives, we will learn to see the light that chases away the darkness in the cracks of our souls. It is up to us to see the mercy provided from above and embrace it.

I may not know where my life is leading me, but I do know who I am and where I have been. With this knowledge, I will accept who I am by following the paths laid out for my character. Through faith, I hope to develop my soul's character into the woman I can identify with from inside myself.

Someday I hope that my story will help to change the lives of many others struggling with life and the challenges within it. Until then, I will continue forward with my own journey, searching for the next piece to my story's puzzle.

Later that Day

"Okay, that sounds good," Gail replied, as she closed the door to her jeep and turned the engine over. It roared loudly with the suspense of the new day. "I will meet you guys at the camp later, but if I don't pick up some groceries for us now, the stores will be closed by the time we leave tonight."

"Yeah, don't you just love Labor Day!" her friend Anneal exclaimed cheerfully.

"Oh, yes," Gail replied, with her sarcasm shining through. "I just love being rushed to get everything done before everything closes. Oh, and not to mention the joys of hosting camp picnics!"

"Oh, you love it and you know it. Otherwise, you wouldn't be here," Anneal pointed out.

"True," Gail agreed. "I'll see you in a bit."

"Okay," Anneal nodded. "Oh!" she yelled to Gail just

The Woodcarver's Hand

before she backed out of the driveway. "Damien and I were thinking that on the way up to see your grandparents tomorrow, maybe we could stop off and pick up Caden. You haven't seen him in almost a month now. You guys are so happy together."

"Really?"

"Yeah, you guys would make a cute couple."

"No, I mean you really want him to go with us?"

"Well, I never mind if he hangs out," Anneal replied. "It is Damien who is a little worried about taking him up to see Joan and Tom."

"Oh," Gail said, thinking about their last trip together. "Yeah, they didn't really seem to like him, but they were blinded by everything else that had been going on. So, with that in mind, I think it would be a great idea to pick him up."

"Great, I'll tell Damien!" Anneal rejoiced. "Have fun shopping!"

Finishing backing out of the driveway, Gail mocked, "Have fun shopping, Gail. I was too lazy to get out of bed this morning to go with you, so have fun all by your little lonesome self."

Picking up her shades and placing them over her eyes, she quickly remembered, "Oh, shoot! I don't have any money! Where am I going to get money today? Oh, I guess I will have to use credit. I didn't really want to use credit, because I didn't want to go all the way to town. But I guess I will have to now. Crap!" she whined, as she flipped on the radio station. "I hate going to town. It will be so busy today!" she groaned, as she turned the radio up louder. "You know, Lord, I know I promised that I would follow faithfully where you lead me, but you could have reminded me to get money last night from the bank when I left early from work. Now I have to go all the way to town and

175

probably be late getting things set up for this evening. What is the point in sending me to town?

"Well, that is all right. I'm sure there is a reason. What happens, happens."

Making a speedy, sharp right-hand turn, Gail headed for the center of town. With her spirits held high, she sang her way through the traffic placed before her. She wasn't one of the world's best singers, so she made sure that she kept the windows rolled shut.

"Oh, who cares," she said. "I hate driving with the windows closed. You can never feel anything when you shut yourself off from the world. If I want to sing with the windows down, I will."

So she rolled down the windows and continued to sing her heart out. She was too content to even notice the strange looks she received from each passerby. Her heart was beginning to fill with anticipation for the new day. Now, she couldn't wait to see what the day had in a store for her.

"Why did you wake up so crabbily? How could you feel like this on such a beautiful day?" she asked herself out loud, but she knew what was plaguing her heart. "Oh, don't do it," she argued with herself, as she saw the sign reading 'ninety south.' "Anneal and Damien are going to kill you if you do."

Tapping her thumb upon the steering wheel, she contemplated the outcomes of her possible actions. Finally deciding, before she could change her mind again, she stepped on the gas and swerved the jeep in the opposite direction she had first intended to go.

"I am so dead!" she screamed out loud, as she headed south to find the one thing missing from her life. "I might as well start making funeral arrangements!" she cried out loud. Pushing the pedal to the floor, she revved up her engine and

never looked back.

It didn't take Gail long to find what her heart kept searching for around each curve and bend in the road. Her eagle eyes caught the glimpse of a figure hiking toward her in the far distance. The figure walked with a casual strut and familiar passion. Though she could not see him clearly, his mere presence created a sense of warmth and healing throughout her body. In her mind, she knew it was her soul's mate.

"It couldn't be him," she said out loud. Prying her sunglasses off, she shouted, "It has to be. It is him! No wonder you have been thinking about him so much! He was coming for you!" she screamed to herself, as she pulled her vehicle off to the side of the road. Her heartbeat pounded excitedly the closer the man bounded to her.

"Hi, I was wondering if I could catch a ride," the clean-shaven man asked with confidence. His neatly trimmed hair sat tucked gracefully behind his ears.

"Well, that depends on where you are headed," Gail responded, as she pondered the man's question over in her mind.

"Well, you see, I knew this girl once who taught me how to live life through my heart and soul."

"Oh really?"

"Yeah, and without her I wouldn't have been able to identify with myself."

"Unh-huh."

"Well, I guess what I am trying to say is that I don't know who I am without her now," he shyly stated.

"That is a really cute story, but what do you plan on doing once you find her?" Gail courageously asked him.

"You see, she offered me this job once. Like an idiot, I turned it down. I was hoping the opportunity was still

available."

"Well, why don't you climb aboard, and we will see what we can do."

"Thank you," *he said, as he took a seat next to her. "I might add that you are the most beautiful lady that I have ever seen."*

"Will you shut up and kiss me already, Caden? We have to get back home before the picnic tonight, or this will be our last moment spent together."

So he did. He kissed her as if it were his first time. And as the day closed in behind them, the mountain pass rising before them painted an array of possible stories to be written about their travels together. The etiolated page began to fill with the beauty of the sun as they continued on their journey home. Their tender hearts lightened as the pale sun brightened with the rest of the awakening day. With each curve rounded, their souls could feel the words flowing from the author's gentle hands. But the decision of which road to follow was left up to their consolidating hearts.

Printed in the United States
31161LVS00001B/26